MARK JUSTICE'S
The Dead SHERIFF

AIRSHIP 27 PRODUCTIONS

Mark Justice's The Dead Sheriff
Zombie Damnation © 2016 Norma Kay Justice

Published by Airship 27 Productions
www.airship27.com
www.airship27hangar.com

Interior illustrations © 2016 Art Cooper
Cover illustration © 2016 Zachary Brunner

Editor: Ron Fortier
Associate Editor: Gordon Dymowski
Marketing and Promotions Manager: Michael Vance
Production and design by Rob Davis

ISBN-10: 1-946183-00-8
ISBN-13: 978-1-946183-00-2

Printed in the United States of America

10 9 8 7 6 5 4 3 2 1

ZOMBIE DAMNATION

*To the memory of my father, Homer Justice, who introduced me to the Duke,
Ken Maynard, Roy, Gene and Lash LaRue.*
—Mark Justice

"After the War Between the States, a new era of lawlessness and brutality spread across the West like a plague. Amidst this evil, a legend was born. An undead avenger clawed his way from the grave to dispense justice to those who preyed on the helpless. This is the story of the greatest lawman who ever lived twice. This is the legend of The Dead Sheriff."

—*The Dead Sheriff's Crusade*, or *The Lawman Who Rose from the Dead* by Richard O'Malley: Beacon Press, Boston, Mass: 1885.

Chapter One

Martin Dugar loved the smell of roasting, human flesh.

Such pleasure wasn't normal. He was well aware of that. But Dugar wasn't what other folks would call normal, either. And he stopped worrying about that a long time ago. The first time he smelled a man on fire was back at the Battle of Gloietta Pass. The poor cuss was Edsel Bullock, a skinny feller from nearby Sante Fe. Edsel, like Dugar, had signed up with the Rebs for the usual reason: free meals and a rifle you could keep after the war was over. Not many of them took the fight seriously. Hell, what did Dugar know of politics? He never owned a slave.

The War became all too real the moment they were fired upon by the Yankees. Dugar and Edsel were crouched behind a green hillock, frozen by the sound of exploding shells and the smell of gunpowder, like brimstone mixed with blood and bowels.

"I didn't sign up for this, Hoss," Edsel said, as he stood and turned to run. A man in a blue uniform appeared on the top of the rise, and he fired his pistol not six feet from Edsel's back. The bullet burst through Edsel's chest, taking a chunk of his heart with it. The powder flash from the Yankee's gun set Edsel's ragged old coat ablaze. Dugar and the Yank both watched Edsel burn. The Yankee looked mystified, frozen. Dugar rammed his bayonet into the Yank's belly. And then, because he enjoyed it so much the first time, he did it again and again. As the Yank slid off the bayonet for the final time, his blood and purple intestines pooling beneath him, Dugar saw the mighty Union army advancing, and the corpses of the 5th Texas Mounted Rifles spread before them.

Dugar ran from the battlefield. He never looked back. Nor did he ever forget the smell of poor old Edsel roasting in the grass. Ever since, he'd made his living on the wrong side of law. Or what laughingly passed for the law in parts of the West. Dugar didn't have to burn people in his line of work. He did it because he enjoyed it. Simple as that.

Like today, for instance.

Dugar and his boys had been casing the depot in Muddy Creek, Texas, for a couple of weeks. If Muddy Creek wasn't the asshole of the world, then it was in that space between the asshole and the ball sack. It was little more than a depot, a mercantile, a couple of bars, a hotel and a church.

And a bank.

It wasn't anything to crow about—barely the size of a couple of privies. It'd get laughed out of a real city like Dallas, or even Damnation, two towns to the West. But it was still a bank. Still, not too many bank robbers were gonna mess with a small-time outfit like the bank in Muddy Creek. There wasn't enough cash. Unless you hit the bank on the day the money train pulled in.

But Dugar didn't plan to rob the bank, at all. No sir. Too much could go wrong once you were inside the cramped space. Dugar was going to rob the wagon that transferred the cash from the train to the bank.

He'd already watched the transfer once, last Wednesday around nine in the morning, from a comfortable spot in the shade from the front porch of the hotel. The boxes were off-loaded to a small wagon pulled by an ancient mule so wobbly, it was a marvel it could haul anything more than its sorry ass. An old-timer drove the wagon while some kid—probably the old man's grandson—slouched half-asleep in the back, cradling a Winchester over his belly. They drove the wagon the three blocks to the bank, where the fat manager with the jiggling tits underneath his dingy white shirt let them in the back door. That was the way things had been done the whole time Dugar had been watching, and near as he could tell, for as long as there had been a bank in this town. The bank manager wouldn't be a problem. Neither would the old man and his slacker grandson.

In fact, Muddy Creek didn't have much in the way of lawmen. A marshal was assigned to the town and six other small communities over an area of roughly eight hundred square miles. He was lucky if he made it to town once a month. There was a part-time deputy, who was also the town barber. He was short and soft, and as fat as the bank manager, even though he smelled worse under the armpits, to the dismay of his customers sitting in his barber chair. He wouldn't be a problem either.

Dugar decided that after he and his boys stole the money boxes, he was going to set the wagon and the boy on fire. Just the thought of it made him lick his lips. He felt a tingle in his groin.

But there would be time to savor the feeling later. Dugar needed to check on his gang. The first few nights he'd put them all up at the hotel. After they got too rowdy, Dugar made them camp in the desert outside of town. It wouldn't do for them to get made before the heist. Dugar stayed in town. He could put on manners and blend in if he wanted to. The problem was he didn't often want to. Sometimes the urge to hurt, to pour the flame to somebody, was too much.

Tomorrow. Just one more day. Then the job would be over. Dugar could do what needed to be done. Get the money. Torch the boy. Maybe the old man, too. He'd never burned a geezer, and he didn't imagine the odor would be nearly as sweet. Still, he found he was willing to try.

After a breakfast of biscuits and ham in the hotel restaurant, Dugar mounted up and rode the five miles to the camp his boys had set up. The terrain was harsh, rocky ground and sparse brush under a brutal sun, making Dugar doubly thankful he stayed at the hotel.

As he got close enough to make out his three men, he realized—not for the first time—what a ragged bunch of coyotes he'd teamed up with.

Big, stout Tommy Fincham sat on a big rock, fanning himself with his hat. His filthy shirt was ringed with sweat stains. Damned fool wasn't smart enough to find some shade. Huevos, short and round, squatted next to Fincham gnawing on what looked like the haunches of a rabbit. Whatever the critter had been, it was sure scrawny. From this distance it looked raw. That didn't surprise Dugar. Huevos was one crazy Mexican. He didn't talk much, but he once told Dugar that his name meant "balls." It was a fitting name. You needed balls as big as wagon wheels if you were going to ride with Martin Dugar.

And none of his men had a bigger set than Pat Kirby. Pat was a skinny little fuck. Looked like somebody who'd work in a bank. Or maybe a preacher from some quiet little place back east. He was barely five feet tall and couldn't weigh no more than a hunnert twenty sopping wet. But he was the meanest, toughest hombre Dugar had ever met. Plumb loco. Pat made Huevos seem normal. Once, back in the Arizona territory, some ranch hand in a bar had bumped into Pat and spilled the little man's beer. Pat smiled real polite-like and ordered another drink. Later, the ranch hand went upstairs with a whore. Pat gave them time to get started, then slipped up to the room. The ranch hand was on top of that whore, just pumping away, when Pat slid his hunting knife into the man's spine. That ranch hand froze up like a statue. He couldn't move or even make a sound. The whore didn't even realize it. She was still wiggling her ass and moaning like she was enjoying it. All that stopped when Pat rolled the ranch hand off of her. He used the same knife to slit the whore's throat while the paralyzed man was forced to watch. Pat then cut out the whore's heart and forced it all into the ranch hand's mouth until the man choked to death on the blood and gristle. Dugar was the one who dragged Pat out of there before the law showed up.

He was glad Pat was on his side.

When Dugar led his horse into the camp, Pat Kirby was throwing his knives at a crude target he'd carved into a cactus. Despite the heat, Pat looked as cool as winter's day.

"Hey, boss," he said. "Ain't it about time?"

"Tomorrow, Pat. Just like I told you."

Pat threw another knife into the center of the target. Fincham stood up from the rock and wiped a sleeve across his sweaty forehead. Huevos tossed away the bone of whatever he'd been eating.

"You two ready to make a little cash?" Dugar said.

"Si," Huevos said.

"Shore," Fincham said. "The sooner we finish, the sooner we can light outta here."

"Look, I know you boys wanted to stay in town, but—"

"It ain't that, Marty," Fincham said. He looked down at the ground. "It's just, well, we heard . . ."

"What?"

"He heard a fairy tale, is what he heard," Pat Kirby said. His back was turned to them as he plucked three knives from the cactus.

"The Dead Sheriff ain't no goddamn fairy tale," Fincham said.

The Dead Sheriff.

Dugar swallowed hard, before forcing a smile onto his face.

"The Dead Sheriff ain't real, Tommy. That's just a story they tell to scare kids and Mexicans. Uh, no offense, Huevos."

Huevos didn't reply. He just stared at Dugar. The Mexican was scared, too.

"Now where did you hear this big news?" Dugar said. He finished his sentence with a little laugh.

"From an old man and his two daughters," Pat said. The little man packed his knives away, one in each boot and a third in the sheath he wore on his leather belt. "They passed through here around supper time last night. They wanted to know if we wanted to break bread with 'em. So we had some nice food and conversation.

"They came from El Paso, and they seen The Dead Sheriff gun down Billy Pecos right in broad daylight. Said he stunk like high heaven and had bits of him fallin' off. The Dead Sheriff, I mean, not Pecos. Said he was so fast with the gun that his dead hand was just a blur, like the devil hisself was pullin' the trigger."

Dugar felt a chill travel from his scalp to his nut sack. Like everybody else, he'd been hearing tales of this dead lawman for at least a year. Too many stories for it to all be made up, even if that's what he wanted his boys to believe. Dugar didn't believe the lawman was really dead. That was impossible. He was wearin' some kind of paint on his face or something. Still, The Dead Sheriff had a good rep for nailing outlaws. Billy Pecos was a tough hombre.

And there was something else nagging at Dugar's thoughts.

"Hold on. This old feller and his girls, they ask what you were doin' out here?" The last thing he needed was some suspicious old-timer flapping his gums back in Muddy Creek, raisin' an alarm and fuckin' up Dugar's brilliant plan. Fincham and Huevos looked at each other and smiled, the specter of The Dead Sheriff momentarily forgotten.

"Over here, boss," Pat said. He walked toward a slight rise in the desert floor. When he reached Pat's side, Dugar saw a small gully, filled with brown scrub brush.

And three corpses.

"Had to shut 'em up, boss," Pat said. "Couldn't let 'em tell anybody about us."

The old man must have been shot thirty times. He was full of holes. The two girls had been cute things. Maybe they were twins. The looked like they were barely in their teens. Their throats had been cut and their dresses were shoved up past their waists.

"Uh, Pat, them girls ain't wearin' underpants," Dugar said.

Behind him, Fincham and Huevos laughed.

"Tommy and Huevos were a little bored," Pat said.

The other two men guffawed.

"Did they relieve their, ah, boredom before or after them girls were dead?"

"Little of both, as I recollect."

Pat had no expression on his face, just like the night he cut out the whore's heart and choked the ranch hand with it. Fincham and Huevos laughed some more. Dugar shrugged. It was better than hearing them whine about The Dead Sheriff.

"Okay, boys," he said. "Live it up today. Tomorrow, you're back at work."

Dugar returned to his mount. He removed two whiskey bottles from his saddlebags. He handed them both to Pat.

"Here's a little treat for tonight," Dugar said. "You show up behind my hotel just before dawn. We'll be rich men before noon."

Fincham and Huevos whooped and hollered. Pat just nodded.

Dugar climbed back in the saddle and headed for town. He wasn't thinking of a bounty hunter who pretended to be a dead man. Dugar was imagining what it would have been like to set those two girls on fire while they were still alive. His cock twitched and hardened in his pants.

⌒⌒

They were in place well before the train pulled into the little station.

Dugar had treated his three men to a fancy breakfast in the hotel restaurant. Or at least as fancy as it got in Muddy Creek. While the others ate and jabbered—mostly Fincham and Huevos—Dugar reviewed the plan in his head. He couldn't see any problems at all. He was a smart and patient man. In a short time, he would be a rich one as well.

Everybody knew their places. Pat sat on a bench in front of the depot until the train arrived and the old man and the kid showed up to load the wagon. As the mule hauled the wagon and its payload away from the station, Pat stood up, stretched and meandered along behind it, just a restless man enjoying a sunny morning in Shitsville, Texas. Fincham and Huevos were stationed behind the bank, just inside a big empty barn that once held a livery stable. Now it housed their horses, one of which was hitched up to a small, light buckboard. Perfect for holding a cash box.

Dugar watched the money transfer from his familiar perch in a big rocking chair on the front porch of the hotel. After the wagon passed by the hotel, Dugar stood and brushed dust from his suit. He stepped from the porch and followed the wooden sidewalk in the general direction of the bank. He didn't have to hurry. Fincham and Huevos knew what to do. Besides, he made sure they stashed a bucket full of kerosene in the old livery stable. After they had the money, Dugar would indulge in a few minutes of pleasure while his boys transferred the money to the buckboard. Then they would hit the trail, rich men all. Of course, Dugar would be richer than the others.

The sidewalk was solidly built. It had just a little give, and he liked the sound it made when his boots hit it. Dugar whistled a happy tune. Things were going extremely well.

Muddy Creek was alive with the typical sounds a small town makes: the murmur of conversation, the buzzing of flies, the steps of horses and humans, the peculiar squeak of one wheel of the wagon as it slowly made its way to the bank.

Then a voice cut through all of that.

"Martin Dugar. Prepare to pay for your crimes!"

Despite the heat of the morning, Dugar's body was instantly chilled. The voice was unlike anything he had ever heard. Deep and sepulchral, it seemed to surround him, coming from everywhere at once. But Dugar knew that couldn't be true. He knew where it came from. Something that sounded like it could only be born from Hell.

Dugar was a practical man. He had never believed any of that Bible stuff his mama tried to teach him when he was a child, right up until the day she was silenced by a bullet during one of his father's drunken rages. Now, as a hardened adult, his mother's teachings rushed back into his mind, called forth by that voice.

He slowly turned. He didn't know what to expect. It wouldn't have surprised him to see Edsel Bullock, the forgotten war casualty from Sante Fe, standing there in the street, his body still burning from the Yankee's gunshot.

What he saw was much worse.

A corpse stood in the center of Muddy Creek's dusty main street.

This wasn't a man in theatrical makeup. This wasn't an actor or a crazy vigilante. The man in the street had been dead for a while. When alive, the man would have been around six feet tall. His hair had been brown. Now it was caked with dust, and much of it was missing. There was a gash on his right temple that was at least two inches wide. The edges of the cut were a dark gray, almost black. White bone shone from beneath the wound. There was no way to tell what color the man's eyes had been. They were white ovals now, with a slight yellowish cast. His mouth hung open, revealing yellow teeth and a black tongue.

The dead man's shirt was old and frayed, and full of bullet holes. Some of the holes had rings around them, as if a little blood had leaked from the corpse. The pants were the color of mud, and the only remarkable thing about the boots was that one of them was planted in a pile of horse shit. Even from twenty-five feet away, Dugar could smell the dead man, like a mixture of rot and sweat and disease.

Despite the tide of panic swelling and burning through his body, Dugar remained still. Watching. Waiting. He noted the fancy leather gun belt the dead man wore and the twin Colt peacemakers in the holsters. Unlike the corpse, the gun belt and pistols were, even polished.

Dugar was conscious of the weight of his own weapon in its holster, a Smith & Wesson Schofield that he had taken off a drunken man he shot for fun a few years back in New Mexico. He felt his fingers drift to the gun's grip before he pulled back. The dead's man blank eyes never looked away.

"You . . ." Dugar cleared his throat. "You got the wrong feller." His voice came out weak and girlish. He hoped none of his men could hear it. But not as much as he hoped he'd make it through this day alive.

The Dead Sheriff did not reply.

"Listen, Mister," Dugar began, before he bit back a bark of laughter. Mister? Well, how did you address a walking dead man? Your Eminent Corpseness? Honored Departed-But-Too-Goddamn-Mean-To-Stay-In-your-Grave?

Dugar swallowed. The street sounds had died away. No one was talking. To Dugar, it seemed that even the flies had stopped buzzing, except for the few now circling the corpse's face. Dugar couldn't look away from those dead white eyes, even though he knew the town was watching and waiting. He couldn't get past the fact that the legend was true, that a walking corpse had tracked him down and stood before him calling him out—a dead man! Dugar had seen some strange things in his life, but how could this be possible? With a swallow, he tried to shove the acrid panic back down his throat.

He quickly considered his options. He could stay and shoot it out. Question was: could he shoot faster than a corpse? Dugar looked the dead man up and down, surveying all the holes in on his rotting body, and he—it—was still standing. Shooting him up might not be the best option. Besides, Dugar preferred to shoot from behind his opponent.

Dugar could run. He had put on a few pounds since his youth, but he was still fast on his feet. The question was: could he find some shelter before the dead man shot him?

The Dead Sheriff was stiff. Waiting.

Dugar had to decide. Act.

Hold on a minute.

Dugar heard that scary voice, then the dead guy was in the street when he turned around. But the dead guy had never moved. Maybe it was all some kind of prank, a joke. Dugar didn't understand it, yet it made a hell of a lot more sense than some deceased lawman riding across the West to track down outlaws. Shit like that just didn't happen. It ain't real. It can't be.

Dugar smiled and dropped his hand to his gun.

Then, the Dead Sheriff's Colt was pointing at Dugar. Just like that. There was barely a hint of movement. One instant the corpse's hand was empty, the next it was full of steel. And the dead man would have shot Dugar, if not for what happened next.

A scream echoed through the street. The Dead Sheriff's head swiveled toward the noise and Dugar could swear the dead guy's neck creaked like rusty door hinges. Dugar followed the dead man's gaze down the street.

The screamer was Pat Kirby. The slight man was carrying a shotgun that was almost as long as he was. It had been leaning inside the big open door of the abandoned livery, waiting for Pat to grab it up when it was time to relieve the wagon of its payload. Pat must have run back there and snatched it when The Dead Sheriff appeared. He was running at an angle to the dead man. As fast as the corpse was, it couldn't adjust its aim before Pat pulled the trigger. The blast knocked The Dead Sheriff off his feet and carried him nearly six feet across the dusty street. The dead man landed in the dirt and didn't move. His dead hand still clenched the Colt. Smoke rolled out of a big hole in his chest.

"Goddamn," Dugar said.

Pat stood on the other side of the corpse. He met Dugar's gaze, and said, "What the hell, boss?"

"I don't know. Why don't you blow another chunk out of him, just in case?"

"Ya think?"

Dugar shrugged. "Hard to aim a gun without a fuckin' head."

Pat broke open the shotgun and dumped the spent shell. He withdrew a fresh one from his pocket, slid it into the breech and shut the action. He stepped carefully over to the corpse. He lifted the shotgun to his shoulder. It looked like a cannon next to his small frame. He aimed at the head.

"Shit! Shit!"

An Injun ran around the corner of the mercantile, yelling. He was dressed in buckskins, and his long black hair streamed behind him. Dugar saw he was young, maybe still a teenager. Not that it mattered. There was a bank to rob.

When the Injun showed up, Pat hesitated.

"Finish it up," Dugar said.

The Injun stopped. He made a gesture with his hand, and Dugar thought he saw a flash, like sunlight dancing off a piece of glass.

The Dead Sheriff lifted his gun and shot Pat in the forehead.

The back of Pat's head exploded. He dropped the shotgun and staggered back a few steps, then folded in on himself, and fell to the street like a bloody sack.

The Dead Sheriff sat up. The big Colt was pointed at Dugar. Dugar could see the door of the barbershop across the street through the hole in the dead man's chest. The fat barber (and part-time deputy) was watching, peeking out behind an old man sitting in a chair.

Dugar looked at the Injun. The young boy's lips seemed to be moving, whispering. A second later, The Dead Sheriff spoke.

"Justice cannot be cheated, Martin Dugar." The jaw still hung open. The lips didn't move as the voice boomed out of the mouth.

Dugar wanted to run away. He needed to be far away from this madness. What was happening here wasn't right. He wasn't a bad man. A little dishonest, maybe, but he didn't deserve this.

But his feet wouldn't move.

It would be okay, though. Fincham and Huevos would show up any second. They would blow this monster to pieces, and that Injun, too. He had something to do with what was happening, even though Dugar would be damned if he knew what it was. Yes sir, Fincham and Huevos were surely on their way. They'd split the money three ways and that meant more time living' the high life before they had to pull another job. All they had to do was get rid of this little problem. This little dead problem.

Dugar looked at the Injun. He was smiling back. He raised his hand and pointed his finger at Dugar like it was a gun. Dugar saw the little flash of light again. The Injun whispered.

The Dead Sheriff raised his Colt, and out of his mouth came the underworld echo of the word, "Asshole." Then it pulled the trigger.

Martin Dugar felt a searing blast of cold, as if he had been stabbed with an icicle, then blackness rushed into the wound and it spread until he was filled with it. The world faded away, and he regretted that he never got to burn the boy on the wagon and the old man.

Fincham and Huevos never showed.

～～

But his feet wouldn't move.

The fat barber was named Aloysius Riordan Slocum. Most people called him Al. He watched the shootout from his barbershop. He felt it was the prudent thing to do. There wasn't much call for deputy work in Muddy Creek and the stipend he was paid went toward a nice meal out now and then or a trip to Sante Fe with his wife. Al didn't wear a gun or a badge unless he had to. After the dead feller shot the two men down, Al opened a drawer behind the barber chair and retrieved the badge. He pinned it on his vest. Then he strapped a holster and a six-shooter around his ample waist. He had to use the last hole on the gun belt. He couldn't remember if the gun was loaded. He got his hat from the hat rack and headed for the door before he realized he still wore his barber's apron. He untied it and tossed it to Pappy Rayburn, who was in the chair, his face still covered with shaving cream. The gunfight had interrupted the shave.

"Pappy, if I don't come back, tell Matilda I love her," Al said.

"If you don't come back, does she know how to shave a man?" The old-timer said.

When Al got to the street, the Indian was helping the dead man to his feet. Like most people, Al Slocum had heard of The Dead Sheriff. And like most people, he hadn't believed the stories.

He was a believer now. That little man blew a hole in the dead feller's chest and then the dead man killed both the shooter and his friend. It was magic or divine justice or the devil's work. Al didn't know which. He didn't really care. He just wanted to help The Dead Sheriff wrap up his business in Muddy Creek so Al could get back to haircuts and shaves, and collect checks that let him take Matilda to Sante Fe, where she always became quite romantic.

When he reached the middle of the street, the Indian had his finger in the big hole in the center of The Dead Sheriff's chest.

"Goddamn it," the Indian mumbled. "I don't know if I can fix this."

"Ex-excuse me," Al said.

The Indian whirled on him, his face clouded with surprise, then anger.

Al ignored him.

The Dead Sheriff stared vacantly down the street. His mouth hung open, and the smell that wafted from his body was like spoiled meat.

"Mister, uh, Dead Sheriff. Sir," Al said. "I'm not really sure what happened here, but…"

"Talk to the Indian." The dead man's mouth didn't move when he spoke. Al tried not to act surprised. He had never heard a dead man speak before. Maybe the mouth wasn't supposed to move.

"Well, sir, as one lawman to another, I'd rather…"

"Talk to the Indian."

"Uh, if you insist." Al turned to face the Indian, who stood holding a wanted poster. Al took it. The picture was a pretty fair drawing of the second man The Dead Sheriff had shot. His name was Martin Dugar and he was wanted for murder and robbery. A five hundred dollar reward on his head, dead or alive.

"You marshal?" the Indian said.

"Yeah. I mean, Deputy Marshall. The name is Slocum."

The Indian just stared at him.

Up close, the Indian was younger than he looked. Maybe eighteen or nineteen.

"You work with The Dead Sheriff, huh? Kind of like his helper? What's your name?"

"Cheveyo," the Indian said.

"Okay. Cheveyo, I assume you'll be wanting this reward?" The Indian nodded.

"Right. Well, the Marshall has to approve it, and he'll be here in about two weeks, I reckon. I'll get some boys to move the dead fellers until…"

He heard the cocking of a pistol hammer. The Dead Sheriff had drawn both of the big Colts.

"Dead Sheriff want money now," the Indian said. "We do job, we get paid."

Al trembled, and the ripple reached his ample stomach, which swished around with the motion of a giant waterskin.

"Now gentlemen, you have to understand my position. There's paperwork and requisition forms and . . ."

"Pay the Indian," The Dead Sheriff said.

Al cleared his throat. "There, ah, are some discretionary funds. I suppose I could get the rest from my savings until the Marshall gets back."

"Good. Pay now," the Indian said.

"S-sure."

The Dead Sheriff holstered his Colts.

"I'll be back in a minute," Al said. He crossed the street to the barbershop. As he walked, he wondered if he had imagined that the Indian spoke pretty good English.

Chapter Two

FROM THE JOURNAL OF RICHARD O'MALLEY:

I am a disappointment to my family.

Father wanted me to become an officer on the Boston Police Department, like him and my grandfather before him (though to be accurate, in grandfather's time it was called the Night Watch and the men—many of them drunk most of the time—carried an odd implement called a hook and bill that was used to cause much damage to both the guilty and those who hadn't been afforded a chance to prove their innocence).

Mother wished that I would pursue a career in the arts, preferably as a painter or poet. She spent long hours reading to me and taking me to art exhibitions, much to Father's chagrin. I suppose between the two of them, Mother is slightly less disappointed in my career choice. A reporter is closer to a poet than a copper.

As to what I wanted, no one ever asked me. If they did, I would have tried to articulate an idea that I barely understood myself.

I wanted adventure. I craved excitement.

From my earliest days, I loved stories of knights and soldiers and heroes, of good versus evil. I believed that was what the world was really like.

But this world doesn't look kindly on children's fantasies.

As I reached adulthood, I turned to the newspaper business under the naïve belief that it was my chance to crusade for the common man, to champion the truth.

My first job was filing police reports for The Boston Examiner. It involved spending the evening loitering around police headquarters and writing up the names of lower class individuals who had been arrested, usually for brawling or petty theft. The names of misbehaving prominent citizens rarely made it into the newspaper. When there was a murder, the Examiner sent a more experienced reporter to get the details, which involved writing exactly what the police told us to write. The one time I dared to question the official version of a story I had been handed, the desk sergeant and two other officers ambushed me behind police headquarters, giving me the thrashing of my young life. If not for my family name, I might have been killed that night.

Suffice it to say, I became cynical about the fight between right and wrong. I drifted through my life, giving my work the minimum amount of attention that was required to remain employed. I became drunk every night after work. I was aimless and cynical. I had transformed into the type of man I had always despised.

Oddly enough, the event that set me on the path to what I believe is my destiny involved a drunken braggart and a legend. I was settled in at my usual stool at Smitty's, a drinking establishment of questionable repute. It was a gloomy spot, which is why I frequented the establishment. I could always drink in peace. At least until the evening when Thunderstorm Parker came to Smitty's.

He arrived in a flurry of profanity and Texas-style whooping (since I had never been to Texas, I took his word on that truly being the source of his war cry). He was the advance agent for a Wild West show that was touring the East. Parker was a wiry man, with deep-set eyes and a face that was so lined by the sun he could have been any age from thirty to sixty. He spent the night telling his mesmerizing tales of the West to anyone who would buy him a drink. I had no intention of participating, but I admit I found the yarns he spun to be entertaining and absorbing. Parker claimed to have known Wild Bill Hickok and, in fact, to have fought beside him in a famous gun battle against the McCanles gang in Kansas. He told of his friendship with Kit Carson and his encounters with famous gunfighters (most of whom, I must admit, I had never heard of). Interesting adventures, to be sure; yet, it wasn't until later in the evening, after Parker's belly was full of Smitty's cheap whiskey, that the rangy Westerner truly piqued my curiosity.

His rough charm had won me over, at least to the point where I added one of his drinks to my tab. Perhaps spotting my reluctance to provide any more free drinks or noting my threadbare garments, Parker took a small sip from the glass.

"Did I mention how things are changing back West?" he said with only the slightest slur to his words.

"You mean with all the new arrivals from back east seeking their fortunes?"

Parker shook his head. "Naw. I mean how law enforcin' is changing."

"I don't believe you've mentioned it."

"Well sir, the West is full of outlaws. That's no secret. But the last few years there's been somethin' new. Outlaw lawmen." "Pardon me?" I leaned forward, unsure of what I had just heard.

"Yep, outlaw lawmen. These fellers take it upon themselves to chase down bank robbers and killers and such and bring 'em in to the real law. Strange business, if you ask me."

"They do this without recompense?" I said.

"Say what?"

"These…outlaw lawmen chase down criminals for free?"

"Oh." Parker took another careful sip. He closed his eyes, as though he was savoring the swill that Smitty served. "That they do. Most of 'em anyway. I know the Lone Avenger does it for free. I think he's rich, anyway—got a big solid gold belt buckle. And I heard every one of his bullets is dipped in gold—even wears a mask that looks like gold. I saw him once, outside Dallas." Parker shook his head. "Runs around with an old Injun helpin' him out. Most of them masked boys got Injuns. I don't get it."

We had moved to a table to better facilitate Parker's admirers. By that late hour, most of the patrons had passed out or moved on to more respectable establishments. We sat alone. I scooted my chair closer to the table.

"They wear masks, you say?"

"Yep. Most of 'em. The Regulator does. And the Coyote Twins. But I get the feeling them two would be dressing up even if they weren't tracking down owl hoots…if you know what I mean. They got a damn Injun, too. There's the Crimson Whip— who has a girl Injun, by the way. Oh, and Señor Spook."

"Who is that?"

"Some asshole that pretends to be a ghost. Wears this white mask that covers his whole head. He ain't no ghost, though. I saw a couple of drunks beat his ass in a bar in Denver one time. He threw up in that mask. It ain't white no more." Parker cackled like a wild animal.

"So none of them claim the bounty of a criminal they capture?"

Parker's gaze darted to his nearly empty glass then back to my face.

"I have time for one more drink, Mr. Parker. Would you care to join me?"

"Don't mind if I do."

Once I secured our whiskies, Parker gladly continued his narrative.

"I only heard of one outlaw lawman who claimed the money." At this point, Parker paused for what I can only surmise to be dramatic effect. "The Dead Sheriff," He said, without a hint of irony or laughter under his breath.

The name sent an electric thrill through my entire body, as though I had reached out to touch Fate.

"Tell me…" I had to pause to draw in a breath. "Tell me about The Dead Sheriff."

Parker's eyes suddenly gained a crafty cast. "I don't know. It's quite a story, an' I been talkin' most of the night. I'm a mite parched."

I didn't care. I would have bought a barrel of whiskey for the man, so long as he told me what I wanted—no, needed—to know.

As soon as I returned to the table with a full bottle and set to filling his glass, Parker found his tongue.

"Let's see, this here story goes back just a few years. Nobody knows his name, but they say this here Dead Sheriff was just like every other man. He was the law in a small town. Some of the stories say it was New Mexico. Others say Arizona or the Wyoming Territory. I guess it don't matter. Anyway, they say the lawman had a beautiful wife and two little girls. He had arrested a troublemaker from a local ranch for killing a man in a bar fight. Some of the other men from the ranch came to the jail to bust out their friend. Not only did they fail, but the lawman shot up a few of them. Eventually, the judge came through and they had a trial and hung the troublemaker. But them other boys at the ranch? They never forgot. They laid low till the hangin' was over, then they went to the lawman's house in the middle of the night. They tied him to a kitchen chair and made 'em watch while they had their way with the wife and the kids before they skinned all three of 'em while they was still alive. The story says the lawman screamed until blood flew out of his throat. When they were done with the females, they started on him. First with hot coals, then with their blades. He lasted until daybreak before he expired."

I felt light-headed. "That's horrible."

Parker nodded as he emptied his glass again. "Yes sir, it was. They buried all of 'em in the town's cemetery, but that lawman just couldn't rest. Under the full moon, he dug hisself out of his grave and went looking for the men who murdered his family. He found 'em, too, up at that ranch, playing cards and laughin' about what they done. The dead man tore into 'em like some kind of mountain lion, I reckon. Bullets couldn't stop him. Nothin' could. I heard those bastards looked like they'd been run over by a train. After that, The Dead Sheriff tried to return to his grave, but they say the cries of the innocent kept him awake. So now he rides wherever he's needed. He lives on for justice." Parker belched loudly. "And fer the reward money."

"Why does a dead man need money?"

Parker shrugged. "I don't rightly know. His Injun does the collecting."

"He has an Indian partner as well?"

"Oh yeah. Well, an Injun helper. Nobody has an Injun partner." Parker looked at me as if I were a simpleton who failed to grasp the most basic facts of life.

I poured a splash of the whiskey in my glass and drank it down. "That's the most ridiculous thing I've ever heard."

"You callin' Thunderstorm Parker a liar?" He seemed more hurt than angry.

"No, of course not. It's just that what you have described is impossible. Maybe there's another explanation."

Parker's brow furrowed and his eyes narrowed to dark slits. "You thinkin' The Dead Sheriff is really Jesus?"

If I had been swallowing at that moment I would have choked. When I could speak, I said, "That's not what I'm saying at all. Rather, could it be possible that this Dead Sheriff fellow is a trickster, perhaps wearing a costume or something?"

"A costume?"

"Yes, and makeup, to make him appear to be, ah, deceased."

"It didn't look like it."

"You've seen this Dead Sheriff?"

"Yep. Didn't I mention that?"

"It must have slipped your mind," I said.

Thunderstorm Parker blinked several times, like a man on the verge of sleep.

"It was in Sante Fe, purt'neer a year ago. I was bendin' an elbow in a saloon with some new friends, when that very same Dead Sheriff walked right into the place. Everything got real quiet, an' the place filled up with this smell like a critter that's been dead for a while. I got a pretty good look at him that night. Parts of his face were missing and you could see the skull pokin' out. His eyes were empty, reminded me of an old Injun scout I knew when I was a pup. He'd had his eyelids cut off by the Comanche and they staked him out for three days in the desert. The sun blinded him and burned all the color out of his eyes. That's what The Dead Sheriff looked like. But he didn't act blind. He walked right up to the table next to mine. He started talkin' in this voice that was deep, soundin' like it was rumblin' up out of a hole in the ground. Like part of him was still in the grave, ya see?"

I nodded, transfixed by Parker's story.

"He told this well-heeled card sharp at the table that it was time for him to pay for whut he'd done or somethin' an' there was somethin' in there about The Dead Sheriff's justice. Believe me, Roger…"

"Richard," I said.

"Believe me, if you had seen and heard this dude, you wouldn't be doubtin' me."

"What happened next?" I demanded.

"What happened was I was hit with the worst case of the backdoor trots that any man had ever faced. I knew that if I didn't run out back to the privy, my britches were gonna be soiled and that was an indignity I wasn't gonna face."

"So you ran?"

"It was more like I ducked under the table then crawled to the back of the saloon. It must have been the steak I had for dinner. I think it might have come from a mule."

"Was there a shootout?"

"Yessir. I heard it from the privy. Coincidentally, my stomach distress cleared up right after the shootin' died down. When I stepped out, I saw The Dead Sheriff walkin' away from the saloon. He had three or four bullet holes in him. And they weren't bleedin.' Not a drop."

I felt off balance, whether from the alcohol or Parker's story I couldn't be certain. I was a man of rational thought. What Parker had just described could not happen. The Dead Sheriff could not exist.

"Have you heard of any Dead Sheriff sightings since your encounter?" I said.

Parker's face was on the table. Drool leaked from the corner of his mouth and he snored like a locomotive.

I left Smitty's and made my way back to my apartment. I was exhausted, yet my thoughts swirled with the speed of a hurricane. I dressed for bed and poured myself a small glass of brandy. The libation was one of two luxuries I permitted myself on my meager newspaper salary. The other luxury was in my hand.

The title of the book leapt from the garish cover. Wild Bill Hickok, or The Fastest Gun in the West. The author was someone named A. P. Dillard, likely a pseudonym. The book was a potboiler, a sloppy combination of fact and fiction that exaggerated the prowess of Hickok to nearly the level of the Gods of Ancient Greece. It was fiction designed to do nothing more than thrill and entertain the masses.

It worked. I was addicted.

While the vices of other men ran toward drinking or gambling, opium or whores, I was a slave to the cheap dime novels that chronicled the lives and times of the Western gunfighters. While I was certainly intelligent enough to know the dramatic exploits of these publications were a fabrication, the tales of adventure sparked my soul.

My evening with Thunderstorm Parker and his stories about The Dead Sheriff fanned that spark into a roaring flame.

For the first time in months I felt alive. I was meant for more than transcribing police reports for the Examiner. I led a life of gray drabness. It smothered me and threatened to make me old before my time. There had to be more than this. There had to be color and excitement, perhaps love and satisfaction.

By the time I finished my brandy I had made my decision.

I would go west.

I would find The Dead Sheriff.

And I would tell his story.

Chapter Three

Ludlow Skaggs was the king of Damnation, and everyone in town knew it.

Especially the Sheriff.

The town paid Sheriff Halwell's salary. Reverend Ludlow Skaggs paid for everything else: the fancy house the sheriff lived in (though not nearly as large or elegant than the right Reverend's own abode, praise Jesus), the nice clothes he and his wife wore, and the other women the sheriff's wife did not know about.

It was a nice working arrangement for everyone involved. The 1,000 parishioners at Skaggs's Church of Eternal Light gave generously every Sunday, and the business owners in Damnation's thriving downtown gave generously once a week to Sheriff Halwell or one of his deputies. That payment insured that each business would be allowed to remain open another seven days. Failure to pay would result in a broken arm or the rape of a wife or daughter. Missing a second payment brought an unfortunate fire or an "Indian attack" that destroyed the building and killed the business owner. Fortunately, that tragedy had only happened once. These days, no one missed a second payment.

The church was a towering structure at the eastern corner of Damnation. Reverend Skaggs ran his affairs (and the affairs of everyone in Damnation; he was a good shepherd, praise Jesus) from a small office in the back of the building. Every few months one of his parishioners would start grumbling about the name of the town being too dark and sinful for the headquarters of the largest church in Texas, and that Reverend Skaggs should do something about it. Skaggs always answered the same way.

"I'm just a country preacher," he'd say, "doin' the Lord's work. But I'll pray our town's fine leaders see their way clear to do the right thing."

What he didn't add was that Damnation's elected officials were hand-picked by Reverend Skaggs and were scared to take a shit without his approval. The name of the town would never change because that's the way Reverend Skaggs liked it. Doing the Lord's work in a place named Damnation suited Skaggs. It made him the underdog in the battle between good and evil. And if he were the underdog, fighting the good fight for the people, then nobody looked too closely into his real job: making money. Piles and piles of money.

Skaggs had tried to make money before, back when he was a kid knocking around the Western territories under a different name. He'd always had ambition in abundance, but he never developed the patience needed to be successful. During one of his many stints in jail, he had done some genuine soul-searching and decided to get into the soul-saving business. It was the best idea he'd ever had. Hard work and a little luck brought him to Damnation and, with a silver tongue and the Bible-learning his drunken grandfather had beaten into him, Reverend Ludlow Skaggs prospered. Grandpappy had not spared the rod, and his lessons from the good book had been remembered.

That was a long time ago. Now Ludlow Skaggs had liver spots on his hands, and his hair was thinning. But he wasn't ready, quite yet, to meet the God he preached about every Sunday. If He really existed, He wasn't going to be pleased with Reverend Skaggs. Best to stick around a few more years and continue his life's work of bringing hope and the fear of the Lord to the townspeople, while collecting every dollar they had, praise Jesus.

"Uh, Reverend?"

Skaggs was startled by the voice. Sheriff Scotty Halwell was seated in the uncomfortable guest chair on the other side of Reverend Skaggs's simple desk. Skaggs had selected the chair specifically for its lack of comfort. He didn't want visitors to stay longer than was absolutely necessary. But Halwell was like a dumb, but loyal mutt. Skaggs was lost in reverie and had briefly forgotten the man was there.

"Excuse me, Sheriff. I had to take a moment for silent prayer."

"Sure," Halwell said. "Anyway, I was just sayin' that collections are good this week. Nobody was short."

"And how is the new man working out?"

Halwell shrugged. His top deputy had been arrested last month in Dallas for killing a man in a bar fight. Reverend Skaggs was a powerful man, but that power didn't extend to Dallas. Not yet, anyway. Skaggs ordered the sheriff to find a new man, someone who would be just as intimidating as the former deputy. Halwell hired a giant of a man named Frye, an apparent scoundrel of some fame in the West.

"My biggest problem is gettin' Frye to keep his hands off folks. Even when the money is there, Frye wants to bust a few heads."

Reverend Skaggs held up a hand to stop the sheriff. "Better to have a horse you have to rein in than one that won't take a step without the whip. Am I right, Sheriff?"

"I reckon you're right, like always." Halwell shifted uncomfortably in his chair.

"Is something else troubling you?" Skaggs said.

Halwell sighed. "I heard The Dead Sheriff was in Muddy Creek a few days ago."

A knot of pain formed in Reverend Skaggs's belly. Muddy Creek was a flyspeck located too close to Damnation.

Skaggs started to speak, but something was caught in his throat. He coughed, then said, "Any report on which way he headed when he departed?"

Halwell shook his head. "No sir. He could be headed to New York or Mexico or Canada for all we know."

Or here, Reverend Skaggs thought. This was troubling. When Skaggs first heard of The Dead Sheriff, he assumed it was a joke or a trick. Over the past couple of years, the sightings and reliable eyewitness accounts had increased to the point that he had to admit something was going on. These vigilantes concerned Skaggs greatly. They were fanatics. They couldn't be bought off. One day, one of these do-gooders might uncover what Skaggs had been doing in Damnation and the right Reverend's little empire could collapse.

But there was another reason The Dead Sheriff worried Skaggs.

If the stories were true, if some lawman had really returned from the dead to punish the guilty, then that opened up a whole new can of worms.

Ludlow Skaggs had always used the Bible as a means to an end—the end being his own financial success. If a man could climb out of his grave to seek vengeance, then that meant all the other stuff—God, Jesus, the devil—was not only possible, but likely. If God were behind this living

"Frye wants to bust a few heads."

dead lawman, then He may be sending The Dead Sheriff here for Skaggs. The thought terrified the preacher and turned his bowels to water. But Ludlow Skaggs hadn't prospered by caving in to threats, even when the threats came from the Man upstairs.

"Sheriff, is my special package safe and secure?"

"Yes sir. The crates are in the vault over at the bank."

Reverend Skaggs smiled. He wouldn't go down without a fight, that was for sure. Skaggs had been concerned about The Dead Sheriff and the other vigilantes for a while. That's why he'd placed an order for a little extra protection, should the moment ever come.

"Good. I want them set up within the hour." He instructed the sheriff as to the locations that would need to be staffed, then sent the man on his way.

Skaggs settled back in his chair. He closed his eyes and examined his situation. If this Dead Sheriff was real—and that was a big if—Ludlow thought that what he had Halwell prepare might be enough to end the grotesque mockery of a man forever. Still, it wouldn't hurt to have another weapon at his disposal.

Vigilantes prospered in the West because of the acceptance of the public. The average man was entranced by the story of a hero that defied the law to protect the innocent. Public opinion kept the vigilantes in business.

Alone in his darkened office, Reverend Ludlow Skaggs smiled. It was a humorless grimace quite unlike the warm, compassionate expression he displayed to the public. This leer would have shocked the white-haired widows in his congregation.

Public opinion was something Skaggs understood. Over the years he had learned to use it for his own gain. And it was time to wield that particular scalpel again.

He withdrew a sheet of fine paper from his desk. He took up the expensive Stylographic fountain pen and began to craft Sunday's sermon.

Chapter Four

In his dreams he still called himself Sam.

And in this dream, he was still a boy, back at the whorehouse.

At first, he saw random images, snatches of memory and half-memory, flashing within his sleeping mind. An emotion was attached to each image.

Fear. Humiliation. Hatred.

The music of his life.

The scenes coalesced into a mosaic of painful memories. Sam was powerless to stop them. He had already lived through them. Wasn't that enough? In one memory, he is with his mother, the half-Indian whore who makes him call her Esmeralda, never Mother. She looks less like an Indian than her son, Sam. He hates the way he looks. It makes his life in the filthy mining town ever more brutal. He is five.

He tries to sleep under Esmeralda's bed while she entertains a customer. The miner is fat and smells like dirt and manure. He grunts like a pig as the bed creeks and the mattress bounces hard above Sam, nearly always banging his head, but somehow always falling short. After the fat man finishes, he calls her a dirty whore and smacks her. Sam is eight years old.

In another, he is beaten by a crowd behind the small saloon in town. His crime was speaking to a white girl his own age. After the men finish kicking him, as he lies gasping in the dirt, the girl walks over and spits on him, then calls him a half-breed son of a whore. Sam is twelve.

One year later, he spies through the nearly closed door of Esmeralda's room. She has aged, thanks to the drinking and the abuse. He hasn't slept under her bed for a long time. She never asks him where he sleeps. She never asks him anything. Sam can't believe what he's seeing. His mother is floating above her bed, seemingly asleep. The man in the room is speaking in some unknown language, words that hurt Sam's ears. The sounds are muted, yet sharp at the same time. The man is naked except for a locket around his neck, and his erect penis bobs in front of him as he dances from foot to foot, chanting. His long red hair floats behind him like he is standing in a storm rather than a dirty room in a decrepit whorehouse. Out of the corner of his eye, Sam sees strange black shadows wiggling in celebration, like an audience at a music hall. When he looks directly at them, they vanish, only to reappear when his gaze returns to his mother and the red-haired stranger. The shapes are angular, like nothing he has ever seen in his thirteen years. The man clutches a book in one hand, a small volume with a shiny leather cover. The words on the cover glow with a bluish light. Sam doesn't know what all of this means. He just knows that the book is powerful, and power means he can leave this little New Mexico town forever. He has to find a way to get that book.

When he awoke, he was sure he was still in New Mexico, still chained to that whorehouse.

The smell of the night air told a different story.

Texas. He was in Texas.

An empty whiskey bottle lay next to the cold ashes of his campfire. His head was still fuzzy from the alcohol and his thoughts were slow. His tongue felt as thick as a sponge.

He smelled the dead man, of course. The magic slowed the decay of the corpse, but nothing could completely halt the process. It was okay, though. He was used to the smell.

He walked a few feet from his bedroll to urinate in the dirt. Then he removed a canteen from one of his saddlebags and drank for a long moment. He still felt haunted by the dream. Sometimes he thought of taking some of the money and boarding a ship for Europe, getting far away from the dusty West and its people.

Yet his dreams would be with him no matter how far he fled. Even whiskey offered no protection from his past.

He reached under his shirt to touch the amulet. Just placing his hand on it was reassuring. He replaced his canteen in the saddlebag and removed a small book. The amulet grew warm against his chest. The unusual lettering on the cover of the book glowed with a soft blue light.

The man who had been called Sam, and now called himself Cheveyo, sat on a rock and waited for the sun to come up.

Chapter Five

FROM THE JOURNAL OF RICHARD O'MALLEY:

Gentle reader, I will not bore you with the mundane details of my journey West. Via train and coach I traveled across the vast expanse of America. As I had never been farther West than Marlborough, those who rode with me probably thought of me as a simpleton, gaping at everything in wonder.

At each stop of my trip I inquired about The Dead Sheriff. It wasn't until I was past the mid-West that I began to encounter anyone who had heard of the undead lawman, and these individuals possessed the barest wisps of details, mostly tall tales that proved useless to my research.

The first substantial report I heard (other than the rambling of Thunderstorm Parker) occurred in Omaha, Nebraska. At a small restaurant across from the depot, I dined with a fellow who was returning from a cattle-buying trip to Texas. He appeared to be a well-heeled, educated man. When he heard of my area of interest, his expression darkened.

"Yes, I've seen The Dead Sheriff," he said. "Twice, in fact."

The cattle agent, whose name was Roger Ebbets, was quite visibly shaken by his encounters. In fact, it took a tremendous amount of persuasion to get him to speak of it at all. Remembering my evening with Thunderstorm Parker, I offered to buy him a drink. That was a waste of money, as the bourbon sat untouched by Ebbets' hand for the entire tale.

"It was nearly a year ago," he said. "I was in Denver on cattle businesses. I don't care for the town. It's easily the most corrupt city I've ever visited." He shrugged. "But I go where I'm told. During that visit I stayed at the Madison Arms, which was rumored to be owned by one of Denver's most notorious criminals. Still, it was the finest hotel I had ever visited. On my first night in town, after dinner, I took a stroll through the business district. The gambling houses and bordellos were doing a brisk business. With all the gas lights, it was almost as bright as noon time. I don't gamble and I don't patronize whores, so I was prepared to make my way back to the hotel when it happened." Ebbets looked away from me for an instant. He cleared his throat before he continued. I was left with the distinct impression that I was conversing with a moral and pious man who was trying to rationalize horrible events he had witnessed. For a brief moment, I regretted urging him to share the story with me. Then, the moment passed and I was an eager listener again, desperate for any detail of The Dead Sheriff.

"I heard a murmur in the crowd. I don't know how long it had been in progress before it caught my attention, forcing me to look to the street. He was walking down the middle of the thoroughfare, covered in shadows where the gas lights did not reach. I still didn't realize what I was witnessing, not until he crossed to my side of the street. When the glare from the lamps struck him, I recoiled in horror. It's not something I'm proud of, but I try to be honest with myself and others. His appearance frightened me.

"His skin was a horrible shade of gray, like a dead animal that has lain in the sun. The meat of one ear hung loose beneath his hat. And thank the good Lord for that hat, for its shadows prevented me from seeing any more of that horrible face. His shirt was full of holes, and stained with what I can only imagine were bodily fluids. Though what fluids were inclined to leak from that monstrosity I didn't wish to contemplate.

"This monster stopped so near to me that I thought I was the object of his attention. My legs seemed to have grown roots into the sidewalk. Had I managed to keep my wits about me, I would have realized I was standing in front of Denver's largest—and most notorious—gambling house, The Silver Nugget.

"Did I mention The Dead Sheriff's mouth? It hung open like the hinge of its jaw was shattered. Yet, he spoke clearly. Frighteningly so. That mouth never moved. He shouted for someone named Tygart to come out and face his justice. That voice was what convinced me I was witnessing something outside of nature. For it carried everywhere. I later learned that people who were at the other end of the main street, half a mile away, at least, heard it with the same clarity as I. The voice may have come out of that walking corpse, but that's not where it originated from. Do you understand?

"This Tygart, as it was explained to me after the event, was the king of Denver's fabled underworld. He or his minions had been suspected in several murders. Unfortunately, any witnesses to his crimes tended to meet an unfortunate demise before a trial could be held. None of that mattered at the time, of course. My greatest hope was to live through what was about to happen.

"Men swarmed like insects from within The Silver Nugget, from the front door and the sides of the grand structure. They were all armed to the teeth and they did not wait for an order to fire. As soon as they saw The Dead Sheriff, the battle began. The first strike came from the pistol of a thin man in a bowler. His shot tore through the chest of the dead lawman and blew out on the other side. That moment is frozen in my memory as though time itself had slowed to a crawl. As the bullet emerged from his back, a spray of black powder erupted from the wound. I say powder simply because that is the word that best describes what I witnessed. I don't know what it was, but it wasn't the innards of a mortal being. The Dead Sheriff staggered from the shot, yet he did not fall. Syrupy drops of fluid, dark as coal and thick as molasses, dripped from the wound. Other shots, fired by nervous hands, missed the dead man.

"Then, The Dead Sheriff pulled his guns.

"I took the only prudent course available to an educated man. I fell to the street and covered my head until the shooting was over. It didn't take long.

"When I looked up again, the street, the sidewalk, the front porch of The Silver Nugget were littered with corpses. Everyone involved in the gunfight was dead. Even the winner. He stood in front of the building, his weapons holstered, immobile as a statue. A young Indian emerged from a building across the street. He hurried to the side of The Dead Sheriff and appeared to conduct a careful examination of that standing corpse.

"If I thought the dead man was quite a sight before the gunfight, I was unprepared for how much worse he now looked. He had been shot through the jaw, and the skin on one side of his mouth was torn away, revealing the jawbone and teeth of a grinning skull. Two of the fingers on his right hand were nearly severed; the digits hung by thin strings of flesh. But the worst wound was a result of the shotgun blast The Dead Sheriff had taken to the midsection. If my skeptical mind still refused to believe the evidence before my eyes, the reality of that gaping mutilation would have been undeniable. I don't believe a cannon could have carved a more destructive swatch through that...thing's body. I could have comfortably inserted my head into that hole, were I perversely inclined. The illumination from the gas lamps threw a flickering skein of shadows over the standing corpse, and perhaps that accounted for what I saw. For it appeared to my eyes that things moved inside that wound, sir. Something writhed and coiled within The Dead Sheriff."

Ebbets grasped my arm with a moist hand. When he next spoke, his voice quavered.

"I wish I could tell you that I bravely stood and bore witness to the aftermath of that supernatural gun battle. Alas, it was in that moment that my courage failed me and I fled like a child. I rushed back to my hotel and locked the door. For the rest of that night I sat in a chair that faced the door with my own Colt in my lap. It was many weeks before I slept well again."

He fell silent. After a moment, my impatience again got the best of me.

"You mentioned a second sighting?"

Ebbets's gaze did not reach my eyes. He remained quiet for another minute. At last, he cleared his throat.

"It was the next day. I was returning from a meeting with my client, a meeting that seemed to drag on endlessly, thanks to my lack of sleep and the ordeal of the previous night. The gunfight was the only thing the townspeople cared to discuss. As it turned out, the criminal Alfred Tygart was among those who had been killed in front of the gambling house. It was said that a federal marshal had arrived that afternoon from Colorado Springs to take charge of the investigation. You see, the Denver constabulary was allegedly as crooked as many of the criminals. This marshal must have decided to conduct business from the police office, for as I walked by that very building on my return trip to my hotel, the door opened and The Dead Sheriff stepped out onto the street.

"He was followed by the young Indian from the night before, who spoke with an older gentlemen wearing a badge, presumably the marshal.

"I tried to hurry past the proceedings, not wishing to relive any of the previous night's events. But as fortune—or bad luck— would have it, The Dead Sheriff stood right in front of me. I was face to face with that abomination. His wounds—the torn flesh, the shotgun damage, the exposed bone—were gone. He was whole again, or as close to it as he could ever be.

"If I believed I was frightened upon first witnessing that shambling monstrosity, that fear paled next to the terror I experienced when I stood mere inches from it. The smell that came from the corpse was almost more than I could accept. My stomach twisted, and the world turned gray. If I had not taken a step back and turned my head in an effort to breathe clean air, I fear I would have fainted."

Ebbets sighed at the memory.

"Mister O'Malley, the longer this conversation lasts, the more damage I do to my ego."

"Think nothing of it," I said. "Lesser men would have soiled their trousers and fled town upon first sighting this creature." As sympathetic as I sounded, I must confess my true motivation was to keep Ebbets talking. I simply had to hear the rest of his tale.

Ebbets glanced at the full glass of bourbon. He licked his lips before he continued.

"The smell was a loathsome combination of rot and age and something exotic, like spices from the orient. By drawing in a great breath, I was able to regain my composure. Or, at the very least, refrain from collapsing. As abhorrent as the beast's smell was, it fairly paled in comparison to its horrifying eyes.

"Those fiendish orbs were as pale as a snow-capped mountain, and as empty as the devil's soul. And, yet, they were not empty. For when I gazed into the eyes of The Dead Sheriff, I saw my own death."

Ebbets turned pale and began to perspire. For once, my voice failed me. I could do little, save pray he continue. After a long pause (and, truth be told, another glance at the drink), he did.

"I know you'll think me mad, and I have questioned my own sanity since that moment, yet the experience was so vivid I can still recall every hellish detail. I was powerless to tear my gaze away from those dead eyes, and the longer I stared into them, the less real the world became. From the corners of my eyes I saw the dusty streets and the buildings waver and blow away, as though they were as insubstantial as clouds. Everything had disappeared, save for The Dead Sheriff. For a time, the rotting lawman and I stood in the midst of nothing. No earth, no sky. It seemed solid ground existed beneath my feet, even if it could not be seen.

"Just as I was sure my mind was lost, the world began to grow around me again. At first it was just the outline of four walls. Slowly the structure gained weight and color. Furniture appeared around me: a bureau, a curio cabinet, an armoire, and several chairs filled with ghostly shapes. I no longer stood. I was prone on a bed. The faces surrounding me gained clarity and I recognized family and friends. My wife Matilda. My sons. The man I work for. At that point I seemed to float toward the ceiling. I turned over and witnessed myself lying in the bed. I was painfully thin, though only a few years older than you see me now. The gray in her hair meant Matilda had also aged: In the bed, I held a cloth to my face, a cloth crimson with blood. As I watched, the Roger Ebbets on the bed coughed violently, and that action caused blood to spray on the cloth and the bed sheets. I was instantly, inexplicably pulled down into the body of the other Roger Ebbets, as violently as if I were tied to a rope that was yanked by a locomotive. The two of us became one, and I was coughing. My chest was crushed by a great pressure. Drawing a breath was a tremendous labor.

"My wife was crying, my sons looked away so I would not see their tears. And there, standing unseen amongst the people closest to me, was The Dead Sheriff, as silent and stationary as a piece of furniture. Those empty, soulless eyes were fixed upon me as I coughed one last time and felt the air squeezed from my body. My heart ceased and the blood stopped flowing. The room—my death room—dissolved into darkness. And I knew no more."

Ebbets suddenly stood. "I died, Mister O'Malley, and I found myself back in Denver, standing nose to nose with that damned mockery of a man. He showed me my death, sir. In a year or five, the consumption will claim me. I am helpless to stop it."

"You can't possibly know that," I said.

He placed the palms of both hands on the table and leaned close to me. "I know, sir. That thing challenged every belief I have ever held, but the one thing left that I truly believe is that the vision he gave me is a true one. Unless you looked into his eyes, you could never understand. I will die, Mister O'Malley. I will die soon. When I do, there will be nothing waiting for me. No Heaven. Not even the flames of Hades. There will be nothing."

Ebbets picked up the glass of bourbon and emptied it in one gulp. He turned away from me, stalking from the restaurant.

When I once again boarded the train, I looked for Ebbets. Either he no longer wished to travel on the same conveyance as me or he had business elsewhere. As the engine began to move along the tracks, I thought about Ebbets's story. The events he had witnessed—or thought he had witnessed—rattled him to the core. Over the course of our conversation, I witnessed the dissolution of his carefully maintained facade until the real Roger Ebbets stood revealed, a man who behaved as if he were dead already.

I knew I should have been frightened, should have caught a train back to Boston.

Instead, I was more determined than ever to seek out The Dead Sheriff.

Chapter Six

"**E**vil is right before our very eyes."

Half the congregation gasped. The other half shouted out "Ay-men!"

Reverend Ludlow Skaggs gazed sternly from his lectern, as if he was daring evil to walk into his church. Inside, he was smiling. You could have your booze or your opium or your whores (and he'd had plenty in his time), but nothing got a man's juices flowing like power, the way he felt it right then, as these people were hanging on his every word, anticipating his next pronouncement.

For Reverend Skaggs, it was glorious. When Skaggs preached well (like today), he felt a connection to the congregation that transcended anything he had ever known. It was so strong that it made him almost believe in something beyond the known.

Almost.

In his mind, he visualized his relationship to his parishioners as that of a golden cord, split into many strands, more intricate than the most complex spider web. The power hummed along that web, flowing both ways, from him to the congregation, then back to Reverend Skaggs again. Their adoration and worship (for beneath all their pious proclamations to the Lord and his boy, it was really Ludlow Skaggs this flock came to worship) was like food and drink to him. Sure, he was in it for the cash. That's why he never told anybody about the jolt he got from preaching. Nobody would understand. At least nobody in Damnation. Certainly not that tin star-wearing dunderhead at the sheriff's office. Halwell was probably the closet thing Skaggs had to a friend in town and that was a goddamn shame. The man was good at making sure the collections were made on time. Other than that, he was good for as much quality conversation as an outhouse door.

Skaggs had paused long enough. After a strong statement, he liked to make eye contact with as many people as he could, from the uncomfortable men pretending they weren't sweating through their coats, to the ladies who fanned themselves vigorously after Reverend Skaggs put an eyeball on them.

He pounded one fist on the lectern while waving his old battered Bible with the other hand. "The evil is in front of us now and many of you do not even recognize it, though its very presence should make you tremble and hide your children!"

He hammered his fist again, a little too hard, truth be told. His arthritis would be screaming tomorrow. But it was worth it. Glenda Perkins, the mayor's wife, was so startled her finely shaped rump actually came up off the pew. The congregation was primed. It was time to bring it home.

"The name of evil is . . ." Reverend Skaggs lowered his voice, forcing his parishioners to lean forward if they cared to hear what he had to say. He was gratified to see that almost all them responded.

"The name of evil is…The Dead Sheriff!" The last three words thundered from his chest, and his heart soared when he saw his audience flinch and throw themselves against the back of the pew. "You know what I'm talkin' about. The abomination. A-bomb-eye-nation! Can I get an Amen?"

Now it was Skaggs turn to be stunned by the chorus of shouts, the exuberance of the response. Skaggs made a show of being so moved he had to wipe a tear from his eye.

"Praise the Lord," he said. "It lifts my heart that you agree with me. The Dead Sheriff is a mockery of life. And that makes him a mockery of the Lord. Do we put up with somebody mocking the Lord? Do we?"

The congregation screamed. It wasn't as organized or dignified as the last "Amen," but there was even more enthusiasm this time. The shouting continued a little too long, and Skaggs knew if he let it continue, he would be in danger of losing control. He laid the Bible on the lectern and raised both hands. He didn't try to speak or shout over the crowd. Within seconds, though, the frenzy subsided.

"Thank you, friends. Thank you for showin' me you see the evil that's heading our way."

Confused mummers burbled up from the pews.

"It's true, it's true," Reverend Skaggs proclaimed. "I have been given a vision by the Lord our God. And in that vision I saw the Beast, and he was shamblin' toward Damnation, and the name of the Beast was The Dead Sheriff."

A few women gasped. The rest of the congregation remained silent.

"I know. I understand. Some of you are frightened. A thing that was once dead, now resurrected. But not resurrected like our savior, Lord no. This resurrection did not come from our father above, did it? Who ordered this resurrection, friends?"

A man in the front row stood up and shouted, "Satan!"

Reverend Skaggs jabbed a finger at him. "Yes, Brother Phelps! Satan lifted that sinner from his grave, and Satan told him, 'Your sinnin' ways are not done. Brush the dirt off of you and go forth into the land and spread my word.' That is what we are dealin' with, friends. The Dead Sheriff is the devil's tool. He…is…an…agent…of…SATAN!"

Skaggs brought both fists down upon the lectern and the old wood boomed like a stick of dynamite, and Christ, did it hurt like hell! They jumped, though—every damn man, woman and child in his church. Mrs. Richey, wife of the bank president, started bawling like a baby.

"But don't fear. We are shielded by our faith in the Lord. It will protect us. For aren't you all soldiers in God's army? He will shelter us against evil, whenever it comes. The Lord's vision did not tell me when. Maybe next month. Maybe next week." He paused again to tighten the noose of suspense around their necks. "Maybe…tomorrow." That did it. Now several women were openly weeping. "But we'll be ready, friends. Together we can ward off the abomination, and tell ol' Satan that this is a Christian town. Can I get an Amen?"

The response was muted, yet heartfelt. He'd rattled them, that was for sure, and he'd shown them who would take care of them. Reverend Ludlow Skaggs was the shepherd in this burg. And it was time to reap what he had sowed.

"Now Sister Gertrude Blaine will come up here and lead us all in the beautiful hymn 'My Faith Looks Up to Thee' while the deacons pass the collection plates. Remember to give generously, friends, for every cent is another bullet in that rifle we got aimed at Satan's head."

Skaggs took a seat while the fattest woman he had ever known waddled up on stage and warbled out the hymn. The deacons had spent the service standing against the walls. Now all six of them grabbed the golden plates and handed them to the person at the end of a pew. Skaggs could see a

"...the name of the Beast was The Dead Sheriff!"

lot of green going into the plates, praise the Lord. The deacons, who also served as Sheriff Halwell's deputies, didn't smile. They took their collecting duties very seriously.

One of the deputies was chewing tobacco as he claimed the plate at the end of one row and passed it to the next. It was the new man, Frye. Skaggs would have to speak to Halwell about him. When the deputies were acting as deacons, they had to display the proper decorum.

As Sister Gertrude hit a note that could drop a mule in its tracks, Reverend Ludlow Skaggs had to work to suppress a smile. This had been a good day. The Dead Sheriff was going to be very good for business.

Chapter Seven

Cheveyo, who still thought of himself as Sam, shifted restlessly on the bench seat of the wagon. He'd bought the wagon nearly a year ago from the widow of a farmer in Arizona. She was selling everything, she told him, and going back east to live with her sister. The price was low and the size was perfect. After all, the cargo he would be carrying was... unique. Over the past twelve months, a lot of dusty miles had rolled under those wheels. He'd made a pile of money and, amazingly, hadn't spent it all on whiskey. Maybe it was time for a better wagon. He wasn't sure his skinny ass could take many more miles in that seat.

Sam heard his cargo shift in the wood-plank bed behind him. He pulled back on the reins and the two horses came to a gentle stop. Sam hopped down, grateful for the break. He untied the leather strings on the canvas cover that protected the wagon's contents. The stench was apparent as soon as he lifted a corner of the canvas. He hardly paid it notice.

He checked on his saddle and saddlebags, the sack that held his frying pan and coffee pot and other supplies. Then he returned to the saddlebags and made sure the book was safe and snug, just where it should be. A man shouldn't have to double-check on the whereabouts of an inanimate object that he'd packed just hours before, but this thing wasn't like any other book. One night he'd fallen asleep with the book under his bedroll, only to find it resting on that uncomfortable wagon seat the next morning. Sam hadn't moved it, and he was damn sure his traveling companion couldn't have done it. Sometimes, he decided, the book just decided to move all on its own, somehow. Sam tried to accept the strange occurrence, just like he'd tried to embrace every damn weird thing that had transpired since he had stolen the amulet and book.

He secured the corner of the cover and went to the other side of the wagon. When he peeled back the cover, he saw the cause of the noise. The dead man had come free of the ropes that secured him to the wagon bed, and his head had repeatedly smacked against the sideboard.

Sam rolled the corpse onto its back and tied it down. The procedure didn't bother Sam anymore. Not like it had at first.

Now, The Dead Sheriff was just another tool, something Sam used in his work. No longer a man, or even a dead man, Sam just thought of him as the puppet, and the thing that allowed him to afford the best whiskey and good steaks and, when he came across a place that would accept Indians, a comfortable bed for the night. The trouble was, of course, those places were few and far between. It was kind of funny, really. If a place would let Sam stay for the night, it was usually a dump he would never voluntarily choose. All because he was a quarter Indian and looked full blood. Hell, he didn't even know what kind of Indian he was. During the few times she would talk about it, Esmeralda claimed she didn't know from which tribe her father had originally hailed.

Yeah, that was pretty funny.

Because, if you let something like that dig its way into your head, you were likely to go just a little crazy and start killing people. And where was the profit in that?

Once he had the corpse tied down again, Sam examined him. The bullet holes were gone, and the left eye had grown back, even if it was still white as a hen's egg. It was amazing what the amulet and the book could do. But they apparently couldn't do it forever. The dead guy was looking worse every day. The wounds took longer to heal. Now the skin had a greasy quality, like it was going to slide right off the bone.

Sam was fairly certain The Dead Sheriff's days were numbered. He would continue to rot away—slowly, to be sure, but eventually there would be nothing left but bones. As scary and impressive as a walking skeleton would be, Sam didn't think it would work. Could a skeleton's fingers even pull a trigger without the muscle and all that other stuff? He supposed he could lash the bones together with rawhide strips or something, though that held some risk. It wouldn't do for The Dead Sheriff to fall to pieces during a shootout.

Hell's Bells, it was hard enough keeping its decomposing ass together as it was. Sam tied down the canvas again. The answer was simple. He had to find a new Dead Sheriff. Maybe not tomorrow or next week, but soon.

Sam shrugged. It wouldn't be tough. He couldn't even remember this one's name.

That's not true.

Despite the heat of late afternoon, Sam shivered.

If you're not going to be honest with even one other human being in the entire goddamn world, at least be honest with yourself.

"No thanks," he whispered.

The voice (he thought of it as Old Luke) didn't answer. Sam conceded that he might remember the name of the dead man who was tied down in the back of the wagon. Still, it didn't matter. Best Sam could tell, he was nobody in life. In death, he was a moneymaker for Sam and his alter ego, Cheveyo. By dying, he had put some bad men in jail and even more in the ground. Half of the West feared The Dead Sheriff. Who wouldn't want that legacy?

And what's your legacy, Sam?

"Shut up," Sam said.

Got a plan for all that money, other than buying whiskey?

Sam sighed. The real Old Luke never knew when to shut up, either.

Maybe spend some of it on whores?

"I hate whores!" Sam screamed. "You know that!"

They weren't all bad, Sam.

Sam stared at his boots. The sight of them wavered. He wiped his eyes before he spoke. "Esmeralda was. And that's the only one that ever mattered."

She mattered, but she wasn't the only thing that did. Remember what I told you. Other people don't make you into a man. You decide the kind of man you want to be.

"Nice words," Sam said. "They didn't do you much good in the end, did they?"

Old Luke didn't answer. It was funny. He hadn't thought of the old man in years. Yet after Sam got a hold of the book and amulet, he started hearing Old Luke in his head. Sam knew it was only his memory, but that voice was sometimes so loud and clear it was like Old Luke was riding shotgun in Sam's skull.

Sam climbed back up on the blasted wagon bench and got the horses headed west. He pulled his hat down securely on his head to keep the sun off his neck. He hated the heat. He'd been born into it, grown up with it, and that should have led him to enjoy it or, at the very least, accept it. He didn't. He hated feeling like he was always baking in a stove. Maybe he should go dig up his money and go east, where it snowed all winter. Or travel as far west as the land lasted and live by this mighty ocean he'd heard about.

Maybe he would one day.

Now he would ride half a day to Drummond.

A bartender back in Muddy Creek gave him a tip. Like a lot of bars, this one didn't serve Indians. At least not where folks could see them. Like a lot places, a redskin could get a bottle out the back door if he paid a little extra. Sam was willing to pony up the cash, and the bartender, who ended up sharing half of Sam's bottle, told him that Crispin St. James had set up a profitable little gambling house over in Drummond.

St. James (Sam was fairly certain that was an alias; real people didn't have names like that) supposedly came from England and had traveled the Orient before coming to America. In the Dakotas, he killed a lawman who'd tried to arrest him for fixing a game. There had been many sightings of St. James over the years. Nothing this close, though. The bounty on his head was large.

Sam showed the bartender a few of the wanted posters he carried in his medicine bag. He only recognized one of them.

"I seen him 'bout two months ago," the bartender said.

The man in the drawing was an ugly cuss named Nelson Frye. He was wanted for killing six men in a bar fight. Barehanded.

"He still in town?" Sam said.

The bartender shook his head. "Naw. D'ye mind?"

Sam handed him the bottle. The bartender took a long swallow before he passed it back. "This here feller was a giant. He said he was looking for work. I told him jobs in Muddy Creek were about as common as a whore in church."

Sam's expression must have been unpleasant.

"Didn't mean to offend."

"Do you know where he went?" Sam said.

The bartender shrugged. Sam gave him the bottle. After another monumental swallow, the man added, "But I told him about Damnation."

"Damnation?"

"Big town, 'bout eighty miles west of here."

"Damnation have a lot of work?"

"It's a thrivin' city, that's fer sure. But this big feller, he wasn't lookin' for regular work. The kind of job he wanted involved bustin' heads. You could tell by lookin' at him."

"So why send him to this Damnation?"

The bartender shrugged again. His speech had thickened, and he had trouble saying certain words.

"Guy hears thangs, y'now? Like if you want to run a bidness in Damnation, you gotta pay the law. If you miss a payment, a guy like this here Frye comes and tears off part of you and feeds it to the hogs."

Sam thanked the bartender and bought another bottle.

He figured to make Drummond by nightfall. Hopefully this St. James cuss would be easy to take down. If things went well, he could be in Damnation by the end of the week. Thinking of the payday that awaited him, Sam smiled.

Chapter Eight

FROM THE JOURNAL OF RICHARD O'MALLEY:

My backside was sore.

Until now, my time on horseback had been limited to childhood birthday parties and Sunday rides in the park with a young lady I courted for several months. By the time I reached Muddy Creek, I was parched, sunburned, dusty and, I was certain, crippled for life. My tailbone was surely broken and my testicles had been smashed as flat as fried eggs.

But it was worth it. I was on the trail of The Dead Sheriff. Two days ago, in a dusty little backwater café, I heard two grizzled and fetid old men comment on the news of the day: a gunfight in a small West Texas town called Muddy Creek. The loser had been one of the seemingly endless number of lawless criminals created by the drums of war. The winner had been The Dead Sheriff. I didn't even finish my meal. The town livery was out of business, so I found a private citizen that sold me a horse, saddle and other supplies. With directions to Muddy Creek, I set out on the trail.

A youth spent in the city is woeful preparation for the simple act of traveling from one Texas town to another. Suffice it to say I survived my trip, discovered Muddy Creek's small, but surprisingly clean hotel, took a room and slept for ten hours. I arose late in the evening, hungry and desirous of human contact. My testes appeared to have regained their former shape, and walking turned out to be much easier than I expected. Sitting, however, was still problematic.

The hotel restaurant was closed, thus I found myself eating a thin steak and drinking bourbon in one of Muddy Creek's two saloons. The food was uniformly terrible; yet, my hunger was so vast I did not care. The bourbon lightened my mood. Suffused with warmth and bad food, I took in the conversation around me. The center of attention was the gangly bartender, dressed in a thin vest and a dirty shirt. His greasy hair was grown long on one side and combed over the balding top of his head. One of the lenses was missing from his glasses. He squinted at the room, whether from nearsightedness or drink, I could not be sure. The other patrons called on the bartender to repeatedly relate the tale of his encounter with some character. Though I was too far from the bar to hear every detail, it was obvious that the story became greatly embellished as the evening grew late and the bartender emptied the drinks the crowd had purchased for him.

After I finished my meal (if such abhorrent slop could be described as such), I took my empty glass to the bar, quickly realizing that the thin, grimy barkeep's story held particular interest for me.

"Did you see The Dead Sheriff, Stinky?" a fat man at the bar asked.

Stinky the Bartender (an unimaginative, yet accurate, nickname) shook his head. "Not so's I could see, but now that ya mention it I...whaddaya call it...I sensed somethin' lurkin' in the dark at the back of that alley."

"Lurkin', huh?" the fat man said. He looked at another man and smiled.

"Shore as my name is Stinky."

Since his name was almost certainly not Stinky, I'm not certain how much veracity his pledge contained.

"What about the Injun, Stinky? What did he want again?" The fat man punctuated his question with a jab of the elbow at his friend.

Stinky hooked his thumbs into the pockets of his vest. "Well, sir, we talked about a great many things, but the gist of it was The Dead Sheriff wanted me on his team."

"What team?"

"There'd be the dead guy, the Injun and me, ridin' across the West, trackin' down outlaws."

"And why'd he pick you?" the fat man said. "He need somebody to pour his drinks after a hard day of outlaw trackin'?"

The gathered assembly roared with laughter. Stinky blinked a few times but did not otherwise react, which gave me the impression he was accustomed to the group's teasing. He finally noticed me.

"Get you something, mister?" he asked. His nose was running. Since he didn't seem to notice or care, I thought it would be impolite to point it out.

"A bottle," I said. The fat man and his half-dozen compadres gave me a hard look, as though I intended to interrupt their fun. I smiled, paid Stinky, and took my bottle back to the table. I drank slowly, listening to Stinky's stories and the raucous laughter of the fat man and his friends.

Sometime after midnight, the crowd dispersed. When Stinky and I were the only two people remaining, I returned to the bar. His head was down on the rough surface off the bar, which looked to have been made from a wooden plank ripped from the side of a barn.

"Excuse me," I said.

"Whuff?" Stinky raised his head from the bar. A tether of snot still connected his face to the wood. This close, his odor was incredibly repellant.

"I need to hear about The Dead Sheriff."

"Naw. It's closin' time. Come back tomorrow."

I dropped several coins on the bar. They landed on the greasy imprint left behind by Stinky's hair. "I'll pay for the information."

Stinky stared at the money before he raised his head to look at me. He squinted so hard that his eyes were nearly closed. I watched him fight for focus and clarity of mind.

"You'll pay me to...talk?" Stinky was one of the rare individuals whose every thought was plainly written across his face. He decided I was crazy, and that a crazy man's money spent as well as a sane man's.

He said, "What do you want to know?"

"The truth," I said.

"Shore, shore. Ol' Stinky'll tell you the truth." He reached for the coins.

I put my hand over his prize. "The real truth. Not that story about you joining up with The Dead Sheriff."

The man visibly sagged. I regretted it, yet saw no other course. If Stinky had information, I needed it. Even if I had to dig a little deeper into my rapidly shrinking savings to do so. If Stinky thought I was a man of wealth and limitless resources, so be it.

"Let's start with what you saw—really—saw. Did you see The Dead Sheriff?"

Stinky shook his head like a schoolboy who has been caught in a lie. A tentacle of drool at the corner of his mouth waved madly as he moved his head.

"Naw. I mean, yeah, I saw him, but it was after the good stuff. The shootin', I mean."

"Did you actually meet the Indian, Cheveyo?"

"Oh, yes sir. The same night. We don't serve Injuns here. Nobody serves Injuns. But I ain't got nothin' against 'em. They never scalped my mama or nothin'."

Stinky laughed like he had uttered the funniest line in the history of the English language. I smiled politely while waiting for him to continue.

"Anyway, this Injun comes to the back door and asks for a bottle, but what he really wants is information, and ol' Stinky has some. I keep my eyes open." He tapped a finger against the side of his glasses that was missing the lens.

"What kind of information?"

"About outlaws, of course. That's what The Dead Sheriff does, you know. Hunts down outlaws."

"So I've heard." I reached into my purse, selected another coin and slapped it on the bar. "Please tell me."

"So I tell 'em what I know, about a slick who's supposed to be runnin' a gamblin' joint in Drummond, and a guy as big as a bear that's workin' in Damnation."

I removed a piece of paper and the stub of a pencil from my jacket pocket. My heart was racing. The alcohol I had earlier consumed seemed to have evaporated from my blood. I was clear of head and eye. I was rich with purpose.

"Stinky, I'm going to need details."

Chapter Nine

The finely dressed man sat across from Reverend Ludlow Skaggs's desk and puffed on a cheroot that was nearly as thick as his wrist.

"You won't join me, Ludlow?" The man spoke through a blue cloud of pungent smoke.

Skaggs didn't like to be called Ludlow. He preferred Reverend Skaggs. The smell of a cheap cigar was not on his list of favorite things, either. He kept his tongue, since he hoped to do business with Owen Lassiter.

"No, thank you. I don't smoke. My body is the Lord's temple, you know."

Lassiter slapped his knee. "By God, you are a character. Everything I heard back in Dallas is true."

"And what have you heard?"

"That Ludlow Skaggs runs a tight ship over here in Damnation. A very profitable ship."

Reverend Skaggs let his gaze drift from the Dallas businessman to the giant who stood with his back against the wall. Lassiter had introduced him as Cleve or Clive or some nancy boy name. It didn't matter. He was almost as big as Nelson Frye. Lassiter liked to travel with a bodyguard. Skaggs decided that was an idea he should appropriate for himself.

"That's nice of you to say, Owen. God bless you."

Lassiter laughed. "You never let up on the act, do you? That's okay. I can respect that."

Reverend Skaggs felt a flush crawl up his neck to his face. Owen Lassiter was quickly getting on his bad side. Sure, the preaching was an act. Still, it was an act that had made Skaggs a rich man. He planned to use it to get even richer. Lassiter was going to help Skaggs with that, whether he wished to or not.

"So how do you know how much to squeeze out of the businesses?" Lassiter took another puff from the cigar as he stared at Skaggs. His tone was friendly, but his eyes held as much warmth as a snake's.

Skaggs's spread his hands apart. "We've worked out a nice system over time, Owen. You take just enough. After all, man still has to make a living. We don't bleed 'em dry. And we keep our word. If they pay on time, nothing bad will happen. It works here. I'm sure it would work well in Dallas. I have been looking to expand my ministry."

Lassiter shook his head.

"You practice such restraint, Ludlow. That's something I can admire in others. Unfortunately, it's not a quality I possess. I don't understand how you can be surrounded by all these profitable businesses and you don't bleed them dry. I couldn't resist. In fact, I won't be able to resist."

Reverend Skaggs straightened in his chair. It felt like the temperature in the room dropped. "What do you mean?"

"You know why I came here?"

Skaggs didn't answer. He had reached out to certain business interests in Dallas in hopes of expanding his growing empire. That plan didn't seem to be working out.

"When I was a boy back in Kansas, my daddy worked on a cattle ranch," said Lassiter. "At the end of the week he and the other hands would go into town to drink and play cards. Harmless fun, I'm sure you would agree. He even let me come along, sometimes. One week there was a new man in town, a card sharp. He suckered my daddy right in, lost some early hands, then he took ever cent my daddy had and some he hadn't earned yet. Humiliated, my daddy pulled a gun on the card sharp. This fellow was ready, though. Had a derringer under the table. Blew off daddy's nuts. He bled to death while the card sharp slipped out the back and disappeared into the night."

Skaggs swallowed.

Lassiter grinned around the cigar.

"The card sharp called himself Lane Stanton. I was just a boy, but I'll never forget that name or the way he looked: the high forehead and thin lips. In fact, allowing for three decades and much good food, he would look just like you, Ludlow. I saw you once, about a year ago, having dinner in Dallas. I decided to find out everything I could about Ludlow Skaggs."

Clive or Cleve or whatever his name was, took a step toward the center of the room, in front of the door. Pulling back the corner of his coat, Clive or Cleve revealed a pearl-handled Colt revolver in a well-oiled leather holster.

"You've done good work here, Ludlow. Do you mind if I call you Ludlow? Or do you prefer Lane? I guess it doesn't matter. You've laid the foundation. Now my associates and I will take over. I don't think you'd like what we're going to do to the place. Of course, you won't be around to see it."

"You've disappointed me, Owen," Skaggs said.

"I imagine I have." Lassiter took the cigar from his mouth. He jabbed it toward Skaggs. "In fact, I'd be a little hurt if you weren't disappointed. It's tough to lose, Ludlow."

"By the way, Owen," Skaggs said, with a pleasant smile on his face. "You're daddy was a stupid drunk and lousy gambler. I'm pretty sure he was a mule fucker, too. Did your mama have exceptionally long ears?"

"You son of a bitch." Spittle flew from Lassiter's mouth. "Do it, Cleve."

So the brute's name was Cleve.

"I don't think Mr. Frye is going to appreciate that," Skaggs said.

The door was thrown open with such force that Cleve was propelled forward just as his Colt cleared the holster. In the tiny office, the shot sounded like the thunder of Armageddon. The bullet went into Lassiter's shoulder. The shooter landed on Lassiter as well.

Nelson Frye had to bend over to fit through the door. Cleve pushed off of his screaming employer, raising his gun toward Frye. Frye grabbed Cleve's hand with a massive fist. He squeezed. Skaggs heard the cracking of bones. To his credit, Cleve didn't scream or wail. He merely moaned. With his free hand, Frye grabbed Cleve's neck. With a sharp jerk, Cleve's neck snapped. Frye turned loose of Cleve, and the would-be killer of Ludlow Skaggs fell to the floor like a sack of feed. Frye turned his attention to Owen Lassiter.

...Clive or Cleve revealed a pearl-handled Colt...

"Get him up," Skaggs ordered.

Frye lifted Lassiter to his feet as though he was carrying a puppy. The Dallas man whimpered. His nice white shirt was stained from his bleeding shoulder.

Reverend Ludlow Skaggs stood up and walked to the front of his desk. He stooped to pick up Lassiter's fallen cigar. He took a couple of puffs from the expensive cheroot.

"Tastes like dog shit, Owen."

"F-fuck you."

Frye squeezed the bullet wound in Lassiter's shoulder. Lassiter screamed, a high shriek that brought a smile to Skaggs's face.

"That's nice, Owen. It's like sweet music. I could listen to it all day." He pulled his watch from a vest pocket. "Unfortunately, the Women's League is expecting me to speak at lunch."

"W-wait," Lassiter said. "We can surely work something out."

Reverend Skaggs puffed on the cigar until the point glowed orange. He thrust the burning tip into Lassiter's left eye. The surface of the eye resisted only for an instant before the cigar sank into the eyeball. This produced a howl that made the man's earlier screeches sound like laughter.

"It's tough to lose, Owen. Not that I would know." Skaggs nodded at Frye. "Kill him quickly."

Frye grabbed Lassiter's neck and snapped it. Lassiter sagged in the big man's arms. It was a more merciful death than he deserved, but Skaggs was pressed for time.

"Put them both in the storage room until dark. Then dump them in the desert."

Frye nodded. He took each corpse by the shirt collar and easily dragged them into the hall. When he was alone, Skaggs saw that Lassiter had pissed on the floor. That made him smile again.

He would go break bread with those fat, braying women from the church. Then he would return here to plan the expansion of his church. Skaggs pictured himself standing upon an altar of gold, spreading his word to thousands. His power would grow and the dollars would flow like a river. From a base like Dallas, he could go anywhere. Even to Washington.

His future was bright, praise the Lord.

Reverend Ludlow Skaggs adjusted his jacket and puffed on Lassiter's cheroot. He was getting used to the taste.

Chapter Ten

Sam rolled the wagon into Drummond around ten at night.

He had ridden through earlier in the day, getting the lay of the land. St. James ran a place called The Lucky Horseshoe. In Drummond, Crispin St. James went by the name of Reginald Smythe. To the townspeople, he was a handsome, sophisticated businessman. To the people who worked for him, St. James was a bloody tyrant with a cruel streak, particularly when it came to the whores who worked the rooms upstairs at The Lucky Horseshoe.

Sam had learned all this from the Chinese kitchen help. They had stayed behind after the railroad was built, and after the lunch rush, they clustered in the alley behind the gambling house, smoking opium and throwing dice. They spoke English pretty well, and Sam knew a smattering of Chinese from his boyhood. He was able to make himself understood.

The workers told him that every night St. James took a different girl up to his private suite on the third floor of the building. From behind the locked doors came terrible screams. If the girl emerged at dawn, she would be bloody and bruised, requiring immediate treatment by the doctor St. James kept on staff. But quite often, the girl did not leave on her own. Two of the hired guns would remove the body wrapped in a sheet, a common sight amongst the Chinese, since the corpse was always carried out the kitchen door.

The cook who told him about the whores displayed no emotion. Like many of the celestials Sam had met, this man accepted that white men held the power in this country, and that many of them used that power to joyously abuse others. It was simply a fact of life, like the sun rising in the morning.

As much as Sam didn't care for whores—hated them, in fact—he realized he loathed Crispin St. James even more. And unlike those women, Sam had the power to change things.

The cook was called Little Five. In some Chinese families, he explained, the children are not given names for several years and were instead referred to by their order of birth. Little Five and two of his sisters had been forcibly taken from their home and brought to America before he could be given a name. He had been separated from his siblings in San Francisco and eventually ended up in Texas. If he was troubled by his forced relocation, or if he yearned for the company of his sisters, he did not show it.

Little Five gave Sam a dish of fish and vegetables left over from lunch. Sam graciously accepted the meal, eating and listening to Little Five talk about the operation of The Lucky Horseshoe. Sam pretended to be looking for work. He wasn't sure if Little Five believed him or simply didn't care. The Chinese man spoke in a soft voice as he squatted in the dust, washing kitchen utensils in a tub of soapy water.

Mr. Smythe always took supper in his quarters at nine o'clock sharp. At ten he emerged to greet his customers. Smythe shook hands and smiled and made pleasant conversation, laughing at the jokes of the gamblers and kissing the hands of their women. After closing, two of Smythe's gunnies carried the night's earnings up to the boss's rooms, where it was counted and placed in the safe. After that, the nightly whore was brought to Smythe.

"That would be the best time," Little Five said.

"Time for what?" Sam asked, after swallowing a mouthful of cold fish.

"To kill him."

The fish grew thick in Sam's throat. Did this celestial know who he was? Sam glanced around the alley. The other Orientals were gambling or smoking. None of them seemed to be listening.

"Why would I want to kill him?"

Little Five shrugged. "Don't know. Just talk. He's a bad man."

"This is Texas," Sam said. "Many bad men."

Little Five continued as if Sam hadn't spoken. "If you could climb the outside of building and go in through the window, you could slit his throat or shoot him while he beat the whore. The closest guard is in the hall, outside his door."

"You have given this some thought."

Still squatting—it seemed to Sam that Little Five could squat like that forever—the oriental said, "I think if my sisters are still alive, someone turned them into whores."

Sam nodded. "All that climbing and going through windows stuff, it's too sneaky for me."

"Indians are supposed to be sneaky."

"This Indian goes in through the front door."

He didn't add: Right behind the reanimated cadaver.

Little Five stared at him for a very long time. "How long have you walked between two worlds?"

"Huh?"

"And when did you lose your shadow?"

Sam turned. His shadow was stretched out behind him, just as it should be. "What are you..."

Little Five walked through the door that led to the kitchen.

He'd been an okay feller until that last bit. Then he sounded as crazy as Old Luke.

Irritated and confused, Sam rode back out to where he had left the wagon, in a little valley full of scrub brush. He tried to sleep, but was troubled by a dream in which a faceless man beat his mother while young Sam hid beneath her bed. He woke up angry and restless. The wait until nightfall seemed endless. To pass the time, he cleaned the dead man's guns and reloaded them.

He uncovered the wagon and examined the dead man's wounds. They hadn't gotten any better.

"What the hell did that mean, walked between two worlds?" Sam said to the corpse. The Dead Sheriff didn't answer.

"There's nothing wrong with my goddamned shadow, either." Just to be sure, Sam checked to see if his shadow was still there.

"Crazy, superstitious Chinaman."

It was dusk. Sam sat on a rock, letting the cool of the evening seep into his bones, as he waited for the darkness to overtake the sun. He knew Indians had all kinds of myths and legends. Esmeralda had mentioned them, and he had heard other stories over the years. He hadn't been raised with any religion or beliefs, other than taking care of his own ass before anyone else. Old Luke claimed to be a preacher, and had tried to teach him some Bible learning. It all just seemed like more rich white guys treating everybody else like shit. Sam didn't have any idea what the Chinese believed.

So why did Little Five's words bother him so much?

The celestial's words tickled something way in the back of Sam's head, buried away. Sam knew it was something that needed to be kept hidden.

Finally, it was dark. He climbed up on the wagon and headed for Drummond. There was a slow rage building down in his gut.

He intended to take it out on Crispin St. James.

Chapter Eleven

FROM THE JOURNAL OF RICHARD O'MALLEY:

Drummond was three times the size of Muddy Creek and it had four gambling establishments. I determined the one I sought through a simple means. I went into the first place, a rather dilapidated business called Smitty's Faro, and asked a few customers if this was the place run by the Englishman. The rather seedy gamblers directed me to a spot on the other side of town called The Lucky Horseshoe, managed by a refined man of British ancestry named Smythe. When I say "refined," I mean that the customers at Smitty's Faro called Smythe "that highfalutin' cocksucker."

I knew I had found Mr. Crispin St. James.

The Lucky Horseshoe was a palace compared to Smitty's Faro. The tables were polished mahogany. The carpet was thick and clean. The dealers were dressed well. So were the whores, although their large and forced smiles could not hide the haunted look in their eyes. I knew the life of a whore was a difficult, often unhappy one. At least it had been in Boston. I assumed it wasn't much better here on the frontier. Still, the women I saw mingling with the customers, touching them on the shoulders and whispering in their ears, seemed to carry a heavier load of sorrow.

Conspiring to blend in, I decided to drink and lose at the faro table. I was determined to pace myself at the former. The latter didn't require any extraordinary effort on my part.

I sipped watery beer and watched my money disappear. The faro dealer—or banker, as he introduced himself—wore a crisp white shirt and a bow tie, and kept up an amiable line of chatter. He seemed genuinely sad when I lost and appeared to be overjoyed on the rare occasion that I won. He was a far better actor than the whores. On the other hand, the dealer wasn't going to spend the evening with one of the players sweating and grunting on top of him.

Shortly past ten, the enigmatic Mr. Smythe appeared. He was perhaps an inch or two under six feet, and carried himself as though he were much taller. He wore a finely tailored suit and had perfectly proportioned features—rather aristocratic, in fact. He was the kind of man that immediately drew the attention of everyone in the room. The women wanted to be close to him. Half the men wished they were Smythe; the other half wanted to kill him. Only the whores were unhappy to see him, though they tried to hide their reaction. Most tried to increase the distance between Smythe and themselves.

He circulated through the big room, shaking hands and laughing at every comment. When he finally made his way to the back of the room and the faro tables, I got the opportunity to observe him at close range.

"Good evening, George," he said to the dealer.

"Good evening, Mr. Smythe."

Smythe worked his way around the circular table. I watched him engage in meaningless chit-chat with my fellow faro players. Now I could see the fine lines around his eyes and mouth. Our Mr. Smythe was older than he appeared. His eyes held a malevolent cast. I know that sounds dramatic, yet after months of covering the police beat back home I had met many career criminals, and the worst of them had those same eyes: soulless, unfeeling, empty. When Smythe made it to my end of the table, he extended his hand.

"Reggie Smythe," he said. "I own The Lucky Horseshoe." "Richard O'Malley." I saw no need to disguise my identity. I thought it unlikely that Smythe was a regular reader of The Boston Examiner's police blotter.

Smythe's eyes narrowed. "That's not a local accent."

"You're one to talk," I said.

"What?" Smythe frowned, and for a brief instant I was permitted to see the real man, the beast that lived beneath the skin. Just as quickly, the smile reappeared. "Quite right. We're both transplants to sprawling Texas. You're certainly from back east. I'd say South Boston."

"That is exactly right." I tried to conceal my surprise. Apparently, my accent was more obvious than I believed.

"Are you here on business or pleasure, Mr. O'Malley?"

"Pleasure. A bit of vacation."

Smythe pumped my hand again, holding it longer than was customary. His cold eyes narrowed again.

"I once knew a policeman in South Boston named O'Malley, a redhead like you. Was he a relative?"

Heat rose to my face. I'm certain Smythe noticed it. Despite feeling as if a rock had become lodged in my throat, I managed to croak out a few words." There are a lot of O'Malleys in Southie. On both sides of the law."

Smythe stared at me a moment longer. At last, he released my hand.

"Enjoy your vacation, Mr. O'Malley, and beware. Texas is somewhat wilder than Boston."

After he walked away, I drained my glass of warm beer. My encounter with St. James/Smythe rattled me. I wasn't sure why. I had nothing to hide. I wasn't here to write an exposé on career criminals or the crooked game of Faro. Still, it was now clear that he had spent time in Boston. Perhaps he had even been arrested by my father. Too bad he wasn't in jail now.

I excused myself from the game. I was exhausted from the hard riding of the past few days. What I needed was fresh air, which would also give me an opportunity to reconnoiter the area for Cheveyo and The Dead

Sheriff. I had no idea when they'd actually appear; yet, I held no doubt they would eventually appear at The Lucky Horseshoe. It was a certainty I felt down in my soul. More than that, I was convinced that meeting the legendary duo and chronicling their adventures had become my destiny. If I had to be in attendance at this gambling establishment every night for a month, I would do it. I no longer had a choice.

As it turned out, my wait was much shorter than expected, thanks to my impetuous nature and innate sense of honor.

As I prepared to exit The Lucky Horseshoe, a commotion drew my attention. Two bearded men, dressed as if they had just left the fields of a ranch, had one of the whores restrained against a wall. One of the men had pulled down the women's dress and was savagely twisting the nipple on her bare left breast. The other man was biting her neck, drawing blood from several places. The whore's screams were ignored by the customers and other employees.

I understand the position of the prostitute in society. They perform a necessary, if ill-regarded function. In a way, they are disposable human beings, condemned to be used and discarded when they can no longer attract paying customers. In fact, (and it gives me no pleasure to admit this) I patronized a prostitute myself in my teen years, at my father's urging. He believed a young man should lose his virtue at an early age so the mind would be free to concentrate on more productive pursuits. I found the experience to be humiliating, terrifying and exhilarating.

Another lesson my father drummed into me was that I could not ignore a woman in trouble. If whores were excluded from this mandate, father failed to mention it. Thus, I entered into the fray.

Though sleight of build, I am quite tall, and from an early age I was trained in the art of fisticuffs by father and his friends. While I never sought physical violence, I did not fear it. However, since I had not been involved in a fight since the age of twelve, I will admit to some slight trepidation.

"Excuse me," I said, clearly and loudly.

Neither man paid me any heed. For a moment, I wondered if the whore was a willing participant in her degradation, screaming to intensify the experience for the men. When she looked at me, I knew this could not be true. There was such a pleading in her tear-filled eyes that I knew I could not hesitate.

I chose to deal first with the biter. I took hold of his shoulder and kicked the back of his knee. He made a noise that sounded like the cry of a small dog. He fell to the floor. I used one of my own knees to strike him on the side of his face. Droplets of the whore's blood flew from his lips. He landed on his side and did not move.

The second man—the nipple twister—released his fleshy prize and launched a kick at my crotch. I managed to twist just enough to catch the blow on my hip. The pain was excruciating. He followed up his kick with a long, looping punch aimed at my head. I blocked it with an upraised arm, and struck his face with the palm of my admittedly large hand. The man's nose flattened under my hand with a crunch that excited my primordial instincts.

The man put both hands over his face and cried, "Asshole. Ya broke my fuggin dose!"

With a growl, he launched himself at me, arms extended to grab me and carry me to the floor. I sidestepped his lunge, snatching a handful of his long hair as he passed by. I used his momentum to swing him around until, off-balance, he tripped over his own feet and landed on the floor. The swift application of the tip of my shoe to his chin ensured that he stayed down.

With both attackers out of commission, I turned my attention to the victim.

"Ma'am, are you injured?"

The whore did the strangest thing. While I did not expect a hero's gratitude from a prostitute, I felt a polite acknowledgment of my actions were in order. Instead, she shook her head at me as one would a child who failed to learn from its mistake. It seemed she viewed me with pity, like I was a simple-minded family member who rarely ventured out of the house.

"Excuse me. Have I done…"

I didn't finish my statement because something struck me on the base of my skull. The blow knocked the sense from me. The room disappeared in a white-hot flash, followed by the deepest darkness I had ever known. I heard, rather than felt, my body hitting the floor. For some time I knew nothing. Then light began to enter my life again, and it hurt. The roaring in my head sounded like a waterfall. I eventually, and painfully, blinked only to see a double vision, the faces of Crispin St. James and Mr. Smythe, now one and the same, looking down at me.

"Still alive? Remarkable. Butch, are you feeling poorly?"

A gruff voice from somewhere behind me said, "I hit him hard as I could, boss."

"You shanty town Irish must have thick skulls."

"Lived…in…a…nice…house," I managed to say. Or at least I think I said it.

St. James glared at me like a feral animal.

"You disrupted my business, O'Malley. You attacked paying customers."

"No…need to thank me."

He barked out a sound that might have been laughter. His face disappeared as he stood up, only to be replaced by the tip of his polished shoe as it flew toward my face.

I awoke the second time as I was being dragged across the floor.

I heard St. James as he shouted.

"Bring that one to me tonight. She's earned it."

I knew he referred to the whore I had foolishly defended.

I smelled fresh air and saw the stars in the night sky. My head bumped against each of the three steps that led down from the entrance to The Lucky Horseshoe. The stars appeared to flare and explode until the night sky was filled with nothing but blackness. I didn't realize I had been unconscious again until I came to as I was tossed to the ground in the alley behind the building. As I lay helpless in the dust, rough hands—presumably belonging to the club-swinging Butch—dug through my jacket and removed my wallet. Before he walked away, he added a kick to my ribs. His heart was not in it, as my bones remained intact.

After several failed attempts, I was able to roll over onto my belly. It took an even longer period of time to work my way to my hands and knees. Then, like a child, I began to crawl. Instinct drove me away from the building, deeper into the alley. I wanted to retreat into the night, to find a safe haven where I could lick my wounds. My head throbbed with agony. I witnessed odd flashes of light from the corners of my eyes, leading me to fear that my brain had suffered irreparable damage. I could only see the dark patch of earth in front of me, since I feared raising my head would cause too much pain. So I continued that way: head down, crawling on all fours.

Until I encountered someone else.

I had traveled perhaps thirty feet, though it seemed farther, when feet appeared before my eyes. The feet were shod in moccasins made of some sort of animal hide. I hesitated, unsure if this was an illusion brought on by my painful stupor.

My breath was coming in great, rasping gulps. I felt I had crawled thirty miles rather than thirty feet.

I steeled myself, and raised my head to look at the rest of the stranger. Limned by moonlight, he appeared to be an Indian, dressed in buckskins. His hair was long and black, and fell around a face that was barely out of its teens.

I knew who it was.

"Cheveyo," I said before I passed out again.

Chapter Twelve

Who the hell was this?

Sam had been standing outside the front of the The Lucky Horseshoe for nearly an hour, watching the flow of townspeople put on airs with their best clothing, men looking to get drunk or get laid, or get lucky at the tables. Or maybe all of them. It was a packed house tonight. Too many white people. If he tried to slip in the front way, it wouldn't take long before his ass was tossed out onto the street. Or worse.

Sam walked around the building. Maybe if he saw Little Five or one of the other celestials, he could get into the place through the kitchen door. He needed to get a look inside, to get a handle on how many men St. James had. The Dead Sheriff (who was tied down in a wagon three blocks away) was pretty fast, but he could only shoot what Sam could see. And the corpse was pretty banged up. It wouldn't do for his gun hands to get blown off by a shotgun. It would be hard to kill St. James and collect the bounty if his gunman had nothing to hold a goddamned Colt with.

So he waited, hoping Little Five would come out for a smoke. The crowd must have been keeping the kitchen staff busy. Not one Chinaman had shown his face.

Sam was prepared to go back to the front of the gambling house, and try to get a good peek through the windows, when a big man in a suit that was too small for him came around the corner dragging someone by the back of the shirt collar. The brute dropped the man—a tall, skinny feller, as far as Sam could tell. The big man riffled through the other's coat, kicked him, and left. The tall man crumpled on the ground, moaning in agony. He was in bad shape.

Sam silently watched him get to his knees and crawl. He moved slowly.

Finally, the tall man made it to within inches of Sam. He looked up and said, "Cheveyo."

The man collapsed face down in the dirt.

How did he know me?

The legend of The Dead Sheriff was growing more every day, thanks to Sam's hard work. He had seen a couple of newspaper articles about the dead vigilante. Both of them mentioned The Dead Sheriff's faithful Indian companion. One of them even referred to him as Cheveyo. Sam was proud of that. He needed a name that sounded more Indian than Sam, and a drunken old squaw back in New Mexico told him it was a Hopi word for monster. Sam liked the irony in that. Old Luke had taught Sam to read, and taught him about irony. Old Luke called it the most powerful force in the universe. Of course, Old Luke was a little crazy.

Sam rolled the tall man over and studied him in the moonlight. He looked like some kind of dandy, with his fancy suit and shiny shoes. He ought to be working in a bank, not crawling on his belly outside a casino and whorehouse. He was probably drunk and a bad loser, so he'd been tossed out on his ass.

Sam left him laying on the ground, and started down the alley. He had work to do and a sizable bounty to claim. He planned to cross the street a couple of blocks down, then work his way back to the front of The Lucky Horseshoe.

But he tripped. His feet became tangled up and Sam went sprawling into a pile of garbage, which caused a hellacious clattering. He tried to stand, but something had him by the ankle. He twisted around, looking back. "Cheveyo," the man said. "Please."

Sam could hear voices and footsteps getting louder. Sam pulled the tall man to his feet, and grabbed him under the right shoulder, leading him down the alley into the darkness between buildings. Holding the man up was like carrying a big sack of mud. After a moment, though, the man recovered.

Instead of going back to The Lucky Horseshoe, Sam led the tall man to the wagon. He made sure no one had followed them, then he addressed the stranger.

"Who are you?"

"Richard O'Malley. You are Cheveyo, are you not?"

"Uh, yes. Me Cheveyo."

"Yes! I knew it!" The tall man had a crazy look in his eyes. "I've crossed the country to find you."

Bruises and bloody cuts covered O'Malley's face. In the moonlight, the blood was just a shade darker than the man's hair.

"Why?"

"I want to write a book about The Dead Sheriff."

Sam was stunned into silence. Old Luke had owned books, but he was the only person Sam had ever known who did.

Sam silently watched him get to his knees and crawl.

"Is he around here?" O'Malley said. He peered around the corners of the wagon.

"Who?"

"The Dead Sheriff."

"Huh? No. He...only appears when evil is present."

"Then you should probably summon him, or whatever it is you do, because that gambling establishment is full of evil."

Another newspaper article would be good for business. But a book? That would mean spending a long time with this man, and there was no way to keep the secret of The Dead Sheriff that long.

"Did you hear me?" O'Malley said.

"No book," Sam replied.

"No book?" The tall man was crestfallen. "But people back east—hell, people everywhere would read this story."

"Go," Sam said.

He walked to the corner of the next building, in order to work his way across the street from The Lucky Horseshoe. O'Malley called after him.

"You speak much better English than I expected."

Sam grumbled as he left O'Malley in the darkness. It was hard to remember to speak the broken English that most white folks expected from Indians. Of course, most of them didn't know any real Indians. For that matter, neither did Sam. The few that he did know spoke better English than most of the inbred cow herders he had met.

Pretending to be someone else was tough. He was still convinced Cheveyo was good for The Dead Sheriff's image, and therefore good for business. The vigilante bounty hunter field got more crowded every day, and everybody had a gimmick and an Indian sidekick. Sam didn't mind playing the part, as long as he kept the profits. It was time to start thinking about the future, though, to do more with that cash than just buying booze. Though he was still a young man, Sam didn't want to spend his life riding across the West with a corpse as his only companion.

He moved to the shadows of a darkened storefront across from The Lucky Horseshoe. The sounds of drunken merriment and tinny piano music poured from the open doors and windows of the gambling hall. A tall, well-dressed man moved through the crowd, greeting the patrons jovially. Sam noticed that the friendly expression faded from his face the instant he stepped away from his paying customers, replaced by the cold look of a snake. Even without the drawing on the wanted poster, he knew this was Crispin St. James. The man carried himself as if the world owed him not only a living, but its worship as well. In other words, this bastard was like every other rich fucker Sam had ever known.

In the darkness, Sam smiled. Every now and then, he was able to mix work with pleasure.

It would probably be easier to take St. James after the casino was closed, but doing it in public would enhance the reputation of The Dead Sheriff. And when it came to humiliating assholes like St. James, the bigger the audience, the better.

He crept through the town and returned to his wagon. Thankfully, O'Malley was gone. Sam pulled back the canvas cover from the wagon and smelled the familiar rot of the corpse. Placing one head on the medallion beneath his tunic, Sam chanted the words from the leather book. The corpse stirred, then sat.

"Go on, climb on out of there, dumb shit," he said. Sam didn't have to speak to animate the corpse. Hell, it wasn't like the dead man could hear him. Sam only had to picture in his mind what he wanted the dead man to do. Saying the words out loud just made it easier to focus.

The corpse obediently clambered down from the wagon and stood in the dark alley. Sam checked the dead man's Colts. Both were loaded and ready to draw.

"All right, let's move out."

The Dead Sheriff walked stiffly in front of Sam.

Directing the reanimated body was practically second nature to Sam by now. He was able to control simple acts—like walking—while thinking of other things. Lately, he wondered if there was a spell in the wizard's book that would keep a gun loaded forever. That would make the bounty hunting a little easier. Picking his way through that book was a long, difficult journey. Only some of the words were in English and the pages weren't always in the same order, forcing him to jump around the book in an effort to find the parts he had already read. A lot of it was trial and error, following instructions and saying the words, sometimes with disastrous results. Like the time he thought he was conjuring up fresh water. Instead, a hole had opened in the night sky over the desert and a yellow fog poured out. The smell of that fog had been horrible. The dead man smelled sweet as perfume by comparison. But worse than the smell had been the skeletal figure dressed in red that peeked over the rim of that hole and glared at him. Its face wasn't like anything he had ever seen. Sam dropped the book and released the amulet. The yellow fog was sucked back into the hole as the opening slammed shut with the crack of thunder. Sam threw up right next to his boots. After that, he didn't open the wizard's book for a very long time.

He stopped the dead man in front of the same store where Sam had earlier observed the gambling hall. Sam cleared his mind. He lifted his arms as if raising a pair of pistols. The dead man mimicked his movement. Sam lowered his arms and the corpse did the same.

Sam again concentrated, this time picturing his voice coming from the mouth of the dead man.

"Horse shit," he whispered.

"Horse shit," the otherworldly voice of The Dead Sheriff thundered. Fortunately, the revelry from The Lucky Horseshoe masked the voice.

It was time to start the show.

Despite the hour, the night was warm. Sweat trickled down Sam's back as he focused on the corpse's actions. He made the dead man walk across the street. Following at a discreet distance, he directed the dead man through the open door of the casino. While he got into place by a window, he let the dead man stand in the doorway for a moment. That was always a crowd pleaser. First, the laughter and loud conversation slowly died away. That was followed by a few whispers and exclamations. Then came the first scream, usually, but not always, from a female patron.

Sam loved that part. Now the real fun began.

He whispered, and the words bellowed forth from the rotting throat of The Dead Sheriff.

"Crispin St. James, prepare to pay for your crimes."

The Dead Sheriff pointed a pale, flaking finger at the well dressed man in the center of the hall.

"There's no one here by that name," St. James said. The man didn't seem startled by seeing a walking, talking corpse at his door. It was time to turn up the heat.

"Your lies cannot fool The Dead Sheriff."

The mention of the name brought the crowd to life. Most of the patrons scampered to the back of the large room, on one side or the other, seeking safety by getting as far away from St. James as possible.

"Boys," St. James said to his men, "show this ruffian to the door."

Three of St. James's hired thugs stepped forward. On the front porch of the casino, Sam mimicked the drawing and firing of twin guns. Inside, the dead man drew for real. The three hired hands fell to the floor with fresh holes in their foreheads.

"St. James, you will now face the justice that will never die," Sam whispered.

He heard the words bellow forth from inside the building, just as a blinding pain exploded in the back of his head. Sam fell to his knees.

What happened? He had to stand up, to direct The Dead Sheriff, but he couldn't move. The agony in his skull drove away all other thoughts.

Someone grabbed a handful of his hair and yanked his head back. The pain in his head intensified. He felt the world fade away. But only for a second. The chill of cold steel against his neck brought him around.

"I don't know who you are, Injun," a rasping voice said, "but you picked the wrong party tonight."

The edge of the knife dug into Sam's neck.

Chapter Thirteen

FROM THE JOURNAL OF RICHARD O'MALLEY:

fter traveling thousands of miles, I finally found Cheveyo, and I'm certain The Dead Sheriff couldn't have been far behind.

But my proposal was rejected.

Oh, I could still write a book, conjured from careless innuendo and fabricated facts, like many of the sensationalist tales that have become so popular. If that were the book I wanted to write.

As you probably have surmised, it was not. I envisioned an accurate history of the undead avenger and his faithful companion, the true story of his miraculous resurrection and dogged pursuit of justice. It would be a tome to cast light upon the revelation of actual supernatural occurrences, and illustrate the theme that the thirst for justice is powerful enough to live on past the death of the flesh.

All I had to do was convince Cheveyo. And at that, I had failed.

After he left me, I wandered aimlessly through the dark alleys of Drummond. The night's heat remained oppressive, but it hardly mattered. I wish I could say the same for the injuries I sustained in the beating. Still, they were nothing compared to the crushing disappointment I now felt. I had spent most of my adulthood being pulled along by events, without daring to impose my will upon the world. I was as helpless as any child and blind to my predicament. All of that changed, thanks to Thunderstorm Parker and his drunken tale of the wandering dead lawman. I had come all this way and exhausted most of my financial resources, only to be denied my request.

I sat for a spell on the front porch of a dark shop, some distance from The Lucky Horseshoe. Only after I sat down did I realize I had chosen to rest at the foot of the local casket-maker. In my forlorn state, that choice seemed like fate, for wasn't my purpose now dead, along with my dreams of adventure? All I had to show for my journey was an empty purse and a battered body.

Looking back on it, I have no doubt my despondency was complicated by my injuries. I had never been one to give up easily, a trait I'm sure would have eventually led me to better assignments with the Beacon. However, on that muggy night, I was weighing my options, which at the moment seemed to consist only of fleeing back to Boston or trying to get a job at a Texas newspaper. I was physically done in, and that malady made my situation seem far worse than it actually was.

Then, an image appeared in my mind. I sat at a table in Smitty's bar, drinking alone, after another evening of drudgery and unfulfilling work. Alone. Always alone. Living a life wasted. Of no use to anyone in this cruel world.

"No," I said aloud. I would not surrender. I would not return to mediocrity or worse, for there were many nights where mediocrity would have been an improvement. I had a destiny in the West, and perhaps it would be my fate to die here. But I made a vow on the steps of the casket-maker's shop. I promised that no matter how my life turned out, no matter the trials and dangers awaited me, I would die a man, with a life well-lived. I was finished sleepwalking through my existence.

Cheveyo may have said no to my request. That didn't mean I was finished asking.

I stood up, emboldened by my newfound passion. I needed to find Cheveyo. The Lucky Horseshoe was where I would start.

I walked down the center of the main street, unmindful of whether I would be seen by any of Smythe's men. I was suffused with such euphoria that I had to restrain myself from singing hosannas. At this point, I must note that I have never been a particularly religious individual, despite— or perhaps because of—my Catholic upbringing. Whatever piousness I possessed when I entered this world had been subsequently beaten out of me by nuns.

Still, as I walked down that street toward my destiny, I felt a connection to the world and to all of Creation. I was part of something much larger than myself, something I would have never experienced had I remained in Boston. There was an energy humming on the stifling night air. Or perhaps it was the ringing in my skull from the beating.

Two blocks from the gambling establishment, I witnessed an amazing sight under a spectral moonlight. With no one else on the street, I saw The Dead Sheriff for the first time. He was dressed simply in a stained shirt and blue jeans. His boots were covered with mud (or, perhaps, mold from the grave). A badge was pinned to his shirt. He walked stiffly, which was not a surprise. I had no experience watching dead men walk, but one could hardly expect them to dance a frivolous jig.

Cheveyo trailed behind the undead avenger.

The Dead Sheriff entered the gambling establishment before the Indian had crossed the street. I heard shouting. As soon as Cheveyo reached the front of the business, gunshots rang out. I saw the Indian move as if he were drawing his own weapons.

However, he did not wear a holster, and I did not see the muzzle flash of a gun. Instead, he stared through the window into the casino.

I increased my stride to a trot. Before I could close the distance, a man appeared from the corner of the building. It was Butch, the man who had accosted me within The Lucky Horseshoe.

He stepped quietly to Cheveyo, producing his short club from within his coat. He struck the Indian, and drove him to the wooden planks of the sidewalk.

I started to shout, then thought better of it. If I were to help Cheveyo, I had to be swift. I ran, my shoes barely making a sound on the hard, dry earth. Each step ignited a jolt of pain in my head. As I neared Butch, I saw the blade in his hand press against Cheveyo's throat. Fearful that I would not reach them in time, I launched myself through the air. My left shoulder struck Butch in the center of his back. At the same instant, I swatted at his knife hand with my right arm. Butch's head rammed into the exterior wall of the building, just under the window through which Cheveyo had been peering. I was unsuccessful at knocking the knife from Butch's hand, although he was unable to cut the Indian's throat. The tip of the blade was driven into the wall, a foot or so from Cheveyo's head.

The blow to his head did Butch in. He fell onto Cheveyo, and I ended up on top of Butch. Hastily, I stood, then rolled the big man off the Indian. I pulled Cheveyo to a sitting position and was about to attempt to revive him when the view through the window distracted my attention.

The Dead Sheriff stood motionless in the casino. His guns were held out in front of him and three men lay dead on the floor. Smythe—or Crispin St. James—still lived. He stared at the undead avenger with a curious expression upon his features. Finally, he walked directly to The

Dead Sheriff. He examined the dead man for a few seconds, as his nose wrinkled with distaste. He slapped the resurrected lawman on the face. So silent was the crowd, the sound of the impact echoed through the open door.

St. James turned to his remaining hired guns.

"Kill him," he said.

"But boss, ain't he already dead?" The speaker was short and round, roughly the shape of a melon. The scars on his face attested to his proclivity for violence.

"Then kill him again, Reynolds."

The round man nodded, pulling his peacemaker from his holster. Several of his men did the same. As if they had rehearsed the act, all of them fired upon The Dead Sheriff at the same instant. The body of the undead avenger jumped with the force of each bullet. As the projectiles exited from his back, a substance resembling thick, black syrup oozed from the wounds. After being struck by multiple shots, The Dead Sheriff toppled over onto his back.

I shook the Indian by his shoulders. He moaned and mumbled.

"Cheveyo, wake up," I said. "The Dead Sheriff needs you."

"Wh…" The Indian's eyes fluttered open, though they were unfocused. He reached for an odd looking locket that had fallen from within his tunic. I was confused about what I had witnessed, yet I felt the connection between Cheveyo and The Dead Sheriff was stronger than I had previously believed.

"He has just been shot down by St. James's men."

Cheveyo's eyes grew large.

"You," he said. "Help me up."

I aided his attempt to rise to a crouch. We both peered into the window. From our vantage point, we could see the torso and legs of the undead avenger. If I turned my head to the right, I could just make out the top of his head protruding from the building's doorway. The hair was patchy, and the scalp was gray and mottled. A wave of unease passed through my body. I was in the presence of the supernatural. Deep in my brain, I felt the urge to flee. It took an effort of willpower to remain where I was.

Four of St. James's men stood over The Dead Sheriff. Reynolds, the round one, toed the corpse with his boot.

"He ain't movin', boss."

"Shoot him again," St. James said.

The four hired guns opened fire on The Dead Sheriff from close range.

The body twitched and jumped. When the shooting stopped a cloud of smoke obscured our view.

"What is that black shit?" one of the men asked. "It shore ain't blood."

"Who cares?" Reynolds kicked the body again. "What do ya want to do with him?"

"Cut off his head," St. James ordered. A woman in the back of the room gasped, and others in the group began to grumble.

"Easy, friends," St. James turned to his customers. "I apologize for this unpleasantness. I was attacked and unjustly accused in my own business. In a moment, play will resume, and I will offer house credit and free drinks to each and every one of you."

The grumbling ended. In fact, a few of the customers actually applauded.

The smoke cleared a bit, and I saw Reynolds shrug before removing a long knife from his boot. He placed the blade against the neck of The Dead Sheriff and started to saw.

Cheveyo whispered. The words were in a language I had never heard. In one hand he clasped the unusual locket. His eyes were tightly closed.

"What are you doing?" I said. "We must go in there and aid him." Even as I spoke the words, I understood what a foolish thing I had proposed. How would two unarmed men deal with St. James, his gunnies and a crowd of gamblers eager for free booze? But my fervor was at an all-time high, and I was determined to help.

Cheveyo did not answer. I peered though the window again, dreading what I was about to witness. Reynolds grimaced with the effort of cutting through the dead man's neck. Sweat ran freely down the fat man's face. Either his knife wasn't sharpened or the skin of The Dead Sheriff was tough, for he had made little progress. The black syrup oozed from a shallow cut beneath the undead avenger's chin.

I failed to understand what had occurred. Had the life force (the vengeance force, as I preferred to think of it) fled The Dead Sheriff's body? Or had some other supernatural force brought about this paralysis upon the dead man?

As I pondered these questions, the fat man ceased his attempt to cut off the dead man's head. He did so because a hand was holding Reynold's wrist, preventing the sawing from continuing.

It was the hand of The Dead Sheriff.

The undead avenger's upper body slowly rose until he was in a sitting position. With his free hand, The Dead Sheriff clutched Reynolds's neck, squeezing through the excess flesh until he found the bone. The snap of the breaking neck was barely audible.

The clientele inside The Lucky Horseshoe were frozen in shock.

As the round man's body sagged to the floor, The Dead Sheriff rose to his feet. Next to me, Cheveyo's strange chanting stopped. He opened his eyes and watched the scene inside as intently as I.

The Dead Sheriff was in bad shape. His body was riddled with bullet holes, thickly encrusted by the dark liquid substance. One of the shots had exited through the back of his skull, leaving an opening only slightly smaller than my fist. Within that wound, I thought I saw movement. Impossible, I know. It was most likely a trick of the light and flickering shadows.

Cheveyo stepped back from the window so he would have more room. He mimed the movements of a gunfighter, drawing his weapons and firing. Inside, shots rang out. Colts in hand, The Dead Sheriff had dispatched St. James's three remaining men. Now the resurrected lawman approached Crispin St. James.

The steady breathing of Cheveyo was the only sound. I chanced a glance at the Indian. His face was calm, but the far away look in his eyes convinced me he was in some sort of trance, like a medium I had once visited back in Boston. That woman had been a fraud, much to the regret of the girl I had been seeing at the time. However, Cheveyo's state seemed genuine. I don't think he would have heard me if I had spoken. For a brief instant there was shimmering movement around the Indian's body. A dark wraith surrounded Cheveyo, a hulking shadow without features. I blinked, and the silhouette disappeared. I decided it was an aftereffect of the blow I had taken to my head. I looked back at the window.

St. James backed up until he was against the bar. The Dead Sheriff stopped about six feet away.

The British man's composure had crumbled. He was wild eyed and frantic.

"Do you think I'm afraid of you?" he shouted. "I survived the worst London had to offer, and I'm still surviving, you bloody bastard."

St. James pulled a Derringer from his coat pocket. He fired at The Dead Sheriff. The small caliber shells did almost no damage to the dead man, as far as I could see. The Dead Sheriff took two steps forward and placed the end of the barrel of a Colt against St. James's forehead.

"No man escapes the justice of The Dead Sheriff," Cheveyo whispered.

"No man escapes the justice of The Dead Sheriff," the voice of The Dead Sheriff roared. A woman in the crowd screamed.

I understood how she felt. None of the stories I heard had prepared me for that voice. Back in Boston, Thunderstorm Parker said the dead man's voice sounded as though it came from the ground, like part of the man was still in the grave. Indeed. But the description didn't go far enough. That voice came from much deeper than any grave. It bore such a quality of eeriness that it could have only originated in the pits of Hades. I had never truly believed in Hell until that moment. All of the nuns' teachings rushed back into my head, and I felt small. Confused as well, for if this power came from Satan, why was The Dead Sheriff fighting for good? And what part did the Indian play here? Cheveyo acted as a puppet master. Did that make him the devil?

Fighting down the urge to flee again, I watched, transfixed as the weird tableau unfolded.

St. James tried to find his voice, though it seemed his mouth had filled with dust. He worked his lips several times, and the best he could come up with was profane.

"Fuck you," he said.

The Dead Sheriff pulled the trigger.

The contents of St. James's skull erupted in a halo of gore. He was thrown against the bar, then, slowly slid down the mahogany until his buttocks reached the floor. His chin lolled forward, displaying the smoking hole in the back of his head for all to see.

The Dead Sheriff turned to the crowd.

"It's closing time," Cheveyo whispered. "Get out."

The order was repeated in the awful voice of The Dead Sheriff. No one in the crowd was inclined to argue with the decree. They filed out, mostly through the back so they wouldn't have to step over any corpses. The Dead Sheriff stood with his guns at the ready until the building was empty.

Cheveyo stood. He drew in a deep breath. When he looked at me, that distant cast was gone. His eyes were clear. He stepped around me to enter the bar. I followed at a distance.

Inside The Lucky Horseshoe, the air stank of gunpowder, coppery blood and voided bowels. As Cheveyo approached The Dead Sheriff, the resurrected gunslinger holstered his twin Colts. "Well, shit," Cheveyo said.

I understood his dismay. The Dead Sheriff was a mess. A bullet had caught his jaw, which now hung open. The right side was completely detached and swung freely back and forth in a small arc. One of the dead man's eyes had been shot out, leaving a deep black hole. The other orb was completely white, as had been described to me. What hadn't been revealed was how that eye seemed to peer into one's very soul. Despite the night's oppressive humidity, I actually shuddered.

"No man escapes the Justice of The Dead Sheriff!"

I took a step back. If Cheveyo noticed, he didn't say anything. He pushed The Dead Sheriff's jaw back into place. It immediately came loose again, swinging like a door with a busted hinge.

There was a commotion outside. A man stepped through the door. Tall and thin, save for the round lump of a belly, the newcomer was busy pulling suspenders over a yellowed shirt. A hastily pinned badge hung crookedly on the front of the shirt. He had obviously been recently roused from his slumber. His cheek bulged with an enormous plug of tobacco.

"Are you shittin' me?" he said to no one in particular. "Is that really him?"

His mouth hung open as he stared at the undead avenger.

"Don't let anybody near him," Cheveyo said, nodding at The Dead Sheriff.

Other than the Indian, the newly arrived law officer and myself, there wasn't anyone else in the casino—at least no one who was alive. Regardless, I took up a position close to the standing corpse. Just not too close.

"You marshal?" Cheveyo said.

"Town constable," the man said. "Dan Nicholson. Is that there The Dead Sheriff?"

Cheveyo nodded.

"I'll be goddamned. He always look that bad?"

"He look better tomorrow."

For the first time, Constable Nicholson turned his gaze from the Dead Sheriff to look at Cheveyo.

"You work for the dead guy?"

"Me Cheveyo."

"Uh-huh."

While standing sentry duty, I wondered about Cheveyo's use of broken English. I now knew that it was an act, but I did not understand its purpose.

Nicholson spat tobacco at a brass spittoon. It splattered on the floor almost three feet from its intended target. The constable walked slowly through the big room (careful, I observed, to skirt a wide berth around The Dead Sheriff). He studied the corpses. When he reached the body of St. James, he squatted next to it.

"I believe this here's an important local bidness man," Nicholson said. "Why'd your boy kill Mr. Smythe?"

Cheveyo joined the constable at the bar.

"Him not Smythe." Cheveyo removed a piece of paper from his tunic. After unfolding it, he passed it to Constable Nicholson. Nicholson

examined the wanted poster of Crispin St. James, then held the drawing
next to the body. He softly whistled. "I'll be goddamned. So Mr. Smythe
was this St. James fellah all along?" He looked up at the Indian. "Did he
and his boys shoot first?" Sam pointed in my direction. "Look at Dead
Sheriff."

Constable Nicholson stood up. He sauntered slowly in my direction.
I stepped away from the undead avenger to allow the lawman an unob-
structed view. As he took in the sight of the bullet wounds to the resurrected
lawman, Nicholson paled. He swallowed. In the process, he must have
ingested a goodly amount of tobacco juice. He sputtered and coughed
before unleashing another unsuccessful attempt to hit the spittoon. He
wiped his mouth with the back of one hand.

"That poor son of a bitch is all shot to hell and back," he said. The
constable glanced at me (mostly, I felt, as an excuse to look away from The
Dead Sheriff). "How is he still standing?"

"His thirst for justice keeps him on this side of the grave," I said. I wasn't
sure where the words came from, but they felt right, and I believed them.

Behind Nicholson, Cheveyo raised his eyebrows.

After studying the wanted poster for a silent minute, Nicholson turned
to face Cheveyo.

"It says five hundred dollars, dead or alive. You want that in paper
money?"

"Gold," Cheveyo said.

"I don't know." Constable Nicholson scratched his chin and looked away.
"See, if ya was to take paper money, I could rustle that up in a few minutes."

"Dead Sheriff want gold."

Nicholson stole another brief glance of the undead avenger.

"What's a dead feller need gold for, anyhow?"

Cheveyo smiled.

"Bullets," he said.

Nicholson contemplated the wanted poster again. He was obviously
reluctant to hand over that much gold to an Indian. Cheveyo walked to
where I stood next to The Dead Sheriff. He grasped the locket beneath his
tunic.

I jumped as the dead man took a step. Nicholson heard it, as well. His
mouth dropped open again as The Dead Sheriff slowly walked over to him.
Behind me, Cheveyo whispered, and I steeled myself for what was about
to happen.

"We'll be back in the morning for the gold."

Constable Nicholson flinched at the ghostly voice. His lip quivered, and he was unable to speak. Feeling some sympathy for the man, I went to him and patted his shoulder.

"Will that be acceptable?"

At first, he only stared at me with a look of puzzlement, like I spoke in a foreign tongue. When my question finally registered, he nodded. He continued to nod as he turned and walked out of The Lucky Horseshoe.

Cheveyo made a sound that might have been a chuckle.

With the excitement of the shootout fading, the smells in the building unsettled my stomach. I walked outside.

A crowd had gathered on the other side of the street. Some of the onlookers had been among the patrons in the gambling establishment. None came closer.

Butch, my assailant, remained unconscious on the sidewalk.

A tremble began in my hands and started to work its way up my arms. Turning my back to the crowd, I crossed my arms over my chest. As violent as life could be in Boston, and despite the fact that I worked the police beat, I had never been exposed to this much death. Oh, I had seen a few corpses, but I had not been witness to the moment of their demise. There was something so sudden and simple about the deaths I had seen tonight. And that simplicity lent the events a casualness that I found unnerving. I suspected that watching the brutal ends of so many men, while witnessing a man who had come back from the grave, would trouble my sleep for a very long time.

I wasn't sure how long Cheveyo had been standing next to me. When I noticed him, I said, "Why?"

"What do you mean?" He kept his voice soft, to prevent it from carrying to the crowd across the street. A glance through the window showed me The Dead Sheriff was still standing inside.

The tremble had traveled to my shoulders and down into my body. I shook like it was February and I was standing at Beacon Hill.

"I don't know. Why…so many things." The chattering of my teeth made conversation difficult. "Why is The Dead Sheriff able to do what he does? Or are you the one who creates the miracle? Why do you speak one way to me and another to the constable? Why am I even here, so far from home? Is it just to bear witness to a slaughter?"

I turned back to the window, drawn inexorably and inexplicably to the nauseating scene beyond the glass. For the longest time, Cheveyo did not speak. In fact, the silence was of such a length that I assumed he, tired of my probing curiosity, had left. When curiosity forced me to look, the Indian was still there. His expression was inscrutable.

He grasped me by the arm and pulled me back toward the door. For one brief instant, I was sure I had witnessed a dark secret, and he meant to murder me for my transgression. Cheveyo had other ideas. He led me to the bar, where I stood a short distance away from the corpse of Crispin St. James. I considered the possibility that I could soon be joining him. Later, with time and reflection, I would realize that the shock of the killings had rattled me to the core. But just then, I watched Cheveyo with curiosity as he went behind the bar and poured whiskey into two glasses. I stared stupidly at the libation he slid across to me.

"Drink," he said. I obeyed. He filled our empty glasses again, and we consumed the soothing liquid. After the third drink, I began to regain my composure. I was even able to relax amongst the bodies and the looming presence of The Dead Sheriff.

"What was your name again?" Cheveyo said.

"O'Malley."

"And you write books?"

"Yes. No. I mean, I am a writer. I work for a Boston newspaper. At least I did until I left Massachusetts. But I am going to write a book about The Dead Sheriff."

The corners of his mouth twitched.

"And what if I say no?"

"Are you planning to kill me?"

"Nope."

I slammed my empty glass on the bar top, and nodded to the half-filled bottle. Cheveyo poured one more round for each of us.

"Then I'm going to write the damn book anyway," I said.

He finished his whiskey and smacked his lips.

"It might be good for business."

"It might? Yes, yes it would be."

Cheveyo leaned on the bar. Four whiskies had put a gleam in his eyes.

"When everybody has heard of The Dead Sheriff, I bet nobody will quibble when I ask for the reward."

"Of course not."

"Hell, outlaws will track us down just to surrender."

"Surely, they will."

"Somebody might even write a song about us."

"They'll write plays about you and The Dead Sheriff," I said. The combination of the alcohol and the emotional toll the day had taken had created within me a state of uncharacteristic giddiness.

Cheveyo lowered his voice. "And what about the women?"

"Women love to throw themselves at a hero. All I have to do is write the true story of The Dead Sheriff and Cheveyo." I held out my hand. I felt this Indian and I had come to an understanding, and as men do, we would seal our arrangement with a handshake.

Except he didn't take my hand.

"Yeah," he said. "We need to discuss that 'truth' part."

I nodded. He feared I would betray a confidence; perhaps reveal a failed romance or an embarrassing childhood incident. Over time, I would make him understand that those topics held no interest to me, save where they led to the path he now rode upon.

"Whatever you say, Cheveyo."

"O'Malley?"

"Yes?"

This time the corners of his mouth did more than twitch.

"You can call me Sam."

Chapter Fourteen

Sheriff Halwell wasn't too happy.

"You're movin' to Dallas?" His eyes were small and bloodshot, and growing angrier by the second. Reverend Ludlow Skaggs had always known his hand-picked enforcer had a temper; that was one of the qualities that made him good at his job. Previously, Halwell managed to keep his anger in check when speaking to Skaggs. That didn't appear to be the case today. In the event the lawman got out of control, Reverend Skaggs kept a tight grip on the gun in his lap.

"Not moving," Skaggs said, in a tone that was reasonable but firm, "expanding. An opportunity has presented itself. I can extend my ministry to many more people."

Halwell snorted. "Ministry? You're talking to me like I'm one of them fat old ladies on the front pew. You mean you're takin' the thievin' business to a bigger town."

Skaggs felt a hot pulse of rage thrum through his veins. He took a breath.

"As I said, I'm expanding my ministry…and all that goes with it. It's a business opportunity. Now why do I have to explain this to you, of all people?"

Sheriff Halwell's face reddened. His breath came out through his bulbous nose in big snorts. This had a good chance of turning bad very quickly. Reverend Skaggs slipped his finger through the trigger guard of his pistol.

"Haven't collections been good for a long time?" Halwell said. "Don't I do everything you ask?"

"Sure you have. That's why you got that nice bonus a couple months back."

Halwell leaned forward in the uncomfortable guest chair, slapping the palms of his hands on Skaggs's desk. The Reverend was so startled, he almost pulled the trigger.

"Then why are you leavin' me here?"

Skaggs was wrong. It hadn't been anger. Not entirely, anyway. Halwell was hurt. And his eyes weren't red from fury. Halwell had been crying like a little girl.

"Leaving you here? Hell, son, you're my key man. I can't make this move without you."

"You…you can't?"

"Of course not. I'm just headed up there for a couple of weeks. Get the lay of the land. Figure our next move. Meanwhile, we've got to keep business going here, don't we?"

"Well, sure."

"And that's why I need my top man running things. Of course, when we're ready to start the Dallas operation, you'll come with me. How do you think you'll like being the top law man in Dallas?"

Halwell swallowed. "I'd like that a whole lot, Reverend."

Too bad it would never happen, Skaggs thought. Halwell had done a good job of shoving the locals around in Damnation, but Dallas was a different story. Skaggs would need someone with intelligence and some political savvy, two qualities that were sorely lacking in Damnation's sheriff. "We're not going to have to hug, are we?"

Halwell's lower lip trembled.

Jesus Christ on a mule. If Halwell started blubbering, Skaggs might go ahead and shoot him now. Frankly, it was only a matter of time. It was obvious Halwell wouldn't react well to being replaced. Reverend Skaggs had a strict policy on dealing with disgruntled employees. He'd probably have Frye do the deed. That boy had no conscience.

"While I'm gone, I need you to decide who will be doing your job once we're set up in Dallas. Whoever you pick needs to start learning the ropes immediately."

Halwell nodded enthusiastically. "I think Hobie Parks would…"

Reverend Skaggs held up a hand to cut him off.

"I don't need to know. Just get it done."

"Yes, sir."

As far as Skaggs was concerned, the meeting was over, but Halwell just sat there.

"Anything else, Sheriff?"

"Yes, sir. It's about The Dead Sheriff."

A ball of fire formed in the pit of Reverend Skaggs's stomach and radiated outward. He had forgotten about the bounty hunter for a few minutes, and that had been a blessed relief. He didn't need this distraction, not when his future was so bright. Skaggs sat back in his chair and rubbed his burning belly.

"Please tell me somebody cut him into tiny pieces and fed him to some hogs."

Halwell's face scrunched up in confusion. "That's not what I heard. He was over in Drummond a couple of days ago." Drummond? Christ, that was less than a hundred miles. He could be riding into town any second. Or maybe he was already here. The burning spread upward to his chest.

"You got men on the buildings like I told you?"

"Sure," Halwell said. "From sunup to sundown."

"What?" Reverend Skaggs was flabbergasted. That goddamned bounty hunter could have slipped into town while they all slept. "I want somebody on those fucking roofs twenty four hours a day."

"But…how they gonna see anything after dark?"

"Torches!" Skaggs bellowed. "Put torches at either end of town. A dozen or more. And keep 'em lit."

"Y-yes-s-sir."

Un-fucking-believable. Did he have to think of every little thing himself?

"One more thing, Halwell." Skaggs tried very hard to keep his voice calm and even. Now his stomach burned from his throat to his belly button, like he'd swallowed a pint of the worst rotgut swill in history. And he should know. In his younger days, he'd drunk enough booze to float the British Navy down the Mississippi.

"Yeah, Reverend?"

"I consider this a serious situation. I'm going to need some direct supervision of the situation."

Sheriff Halwell appeared to be puzzled.

"Uh, you mean you're gonna take a shift?"

"No, dumbass," Skaggs said. "I mean you are."

"Me?" Halwell paled. The man lived a comfortable life, thanks to Reverend Ludlow Skaggs. Unfortunately, Skaggs needed the sheriff to get his hands dirty.

"Drop everything else. Get every man you got up there."

"Okay. I mean, yes, sir."

"This bounty hunter will not ruin my plans...our plans, Halwell."

Halwell stood up. He straightened the lapels of his coat in a futile effort to look dignified. Skaggs let him get to the door before he stopped the sheriff with his final comments.

"If any one of your men gets drunk on duty or falls asleep, I'll have his ass dragged into this very room, and in front of you and God, I will personally cut his balls off. You got that?"

"Got it," Halwell said. The words came out in something quite like the squeaking voice of a boy.

"Good. Don't fuck this up."

Halwell left, softly closing the door behind him.

Reverend Skaggs tried to relax, but the thought of The Dead Sheriff being this close or, possibly, already in town, had him torn up.

"Fuck that bounty hunter," he said to the empty room. He kept calling him the bounty hunter because that sounded normal. Human. It kept him from dwelling on the stories he'd heard, the rumors that this thing was actually an abomination that had risen from the grave.

"Bullshit."

Ludlow Skaggs wasn't going to accept that. Only one man had ever come back from the dead, and the good Reverend wasn't sure he really believed that story, either. So he would proceed with the original plan. He was going to treat this Dead Sheriff just like he was a flesh and blood hombre in a fancy costume.

Not that it mattered. Dead or alive, there wasn't anything that could survive what he had planned for this vigilante. The Dead Sheriff would soon be relegated to the musty pages of history.

Meanwhile, the legend of Reverend Ludlow Skaggs was just beginning. Soon, he would spread the word to Dallas, then further east. He would be the most famous preacher in the history of religion.

And the richest.

Skaggs felt inspired, praise the Lord. Maybe what Damnation needed was a special church service. Evil would soon be upon them, and it was a good idea to remind his parishioners who they must always turn to when it came to the battle for their very souls.

The burning in his stomach was almost gone.

Reverend Skaggs took up his fountain pen and began a new sermon.

Chapter Fifteen

Sam looked at the gangly man on the other side of the campfire, and thought, Why am I doing this?

He hadn't told this O'Malley that he could ride with them and collect information for his book, but he might as well have. He had never let anybody come back to camp with him and the dead man, not even a woman (not that any females were volunteering for a night under the stars with an Indian and a rotting corpse).

On the other hand, no one had ever saved his life before. If O'Malley hadn't followed him to The Lucky Horseshoe, St. James's man would have finished the job, and Sam would be in a hole in the ground—if they even gave a real burial to Indians around here.

He shivered at the thought of being in a grave. Then, in a flash, the memory came.

The wind wouldn't stop and the night sky was alive with strange lighting and the ground opened up and the dead man crawled out, reaching for him with pale, muddy fingers.

It was peculiar, and nothing he would ever talk about, but as much as he had been around death—working with it, living with it, even causing it—it terrified him. He didn't want to spend his life chasing around killers and horse thieves.

Also, he hated feeling obliged to someone. It was his hope he could throw a few facts to this O'Malley and urge him to hit the trail, but he suspected it wasn't going to be that easy.

After the shootout at The Lucky Horseshoe, Sam brought the writer to his camp just outside of town. The tall man fell asleep before Sam had the fire going. While he slept, Sam squatted by the fire and nursed the bottle of whiskey he'd smuggled from the bar. Sam didn't sleep a lot these days, especially when he used the amulet. When he did drift off for a few moments, his dreams were filled with thick darkness, as though he were drowning in an ocean of black. He discovered that if he drank enough, he could sleep without dreams.

Before he became too drunk to stand, Sam took the amulet in one hand, and the leather book in the other. He went to the wagon and pulled back the canvas.

"Shit, you look terrible," he said to the dead man.

Enough light from the fire reached this far to allow him to see the words in the book, the words that moved and danced on the page. Sometimes they were in English. Other times they melted into some kind of language that didn't look like any kind of writing he had ever seen, the letters curving in ways that were just wrong. Obscene. When the book was like that, it hurt his eyes to look at it. Tonight, thankfully, the words were in English, and therefore safe. He read the spell, carefully pronouncing each word. The book grew warm, emitting a foul odor that burned his nose and mouth. When he finished, he pulled the canvas cover back over the wagon bed. It would take time to close up some of those wounds. Sam didn't expect much. Each time he performed the healing spell on the dead man, it seemed to do less.

The next morning, he had to shake O'Malley to awaken him. Maybe it had something to do with his head injury. As the writer mumbled and drooled his way to wakefulness, Sam fretted that he might end up brain damaged, a helpless invalid. If that happened, Sam planned to do the merciful thing and shoot O'Malley in the head. But the tall man woke up cheerfully, especially after a couple of cups of Sam's coffee and a biscuit. "Can I come with you to pick up the reward?" O'Malley asked.

Sam eyed him suspiciously.

"You thinkin' you're owed a cut?"

"What? No!" There was genuine surprise on the writer's face, and Sam relaxed a bit. "I want to see how it happens. Research, you know, for the book."

"Sure. You can come. Just keep quiet. I do all the talking."

"Okay, fine," O'Malley agreed.

He must have interpreted just be quiet as just be quiet when we're collecting the money, for he kept up a ceaseless prattle as they rode the wagon into town. He asked a lot of questions, none of which Sam answered. He had spent the past few years on his own, if you didn't count the dead man. And Sam didn't. In one respect, the dead man was a good traveling companion because he didn't talk.

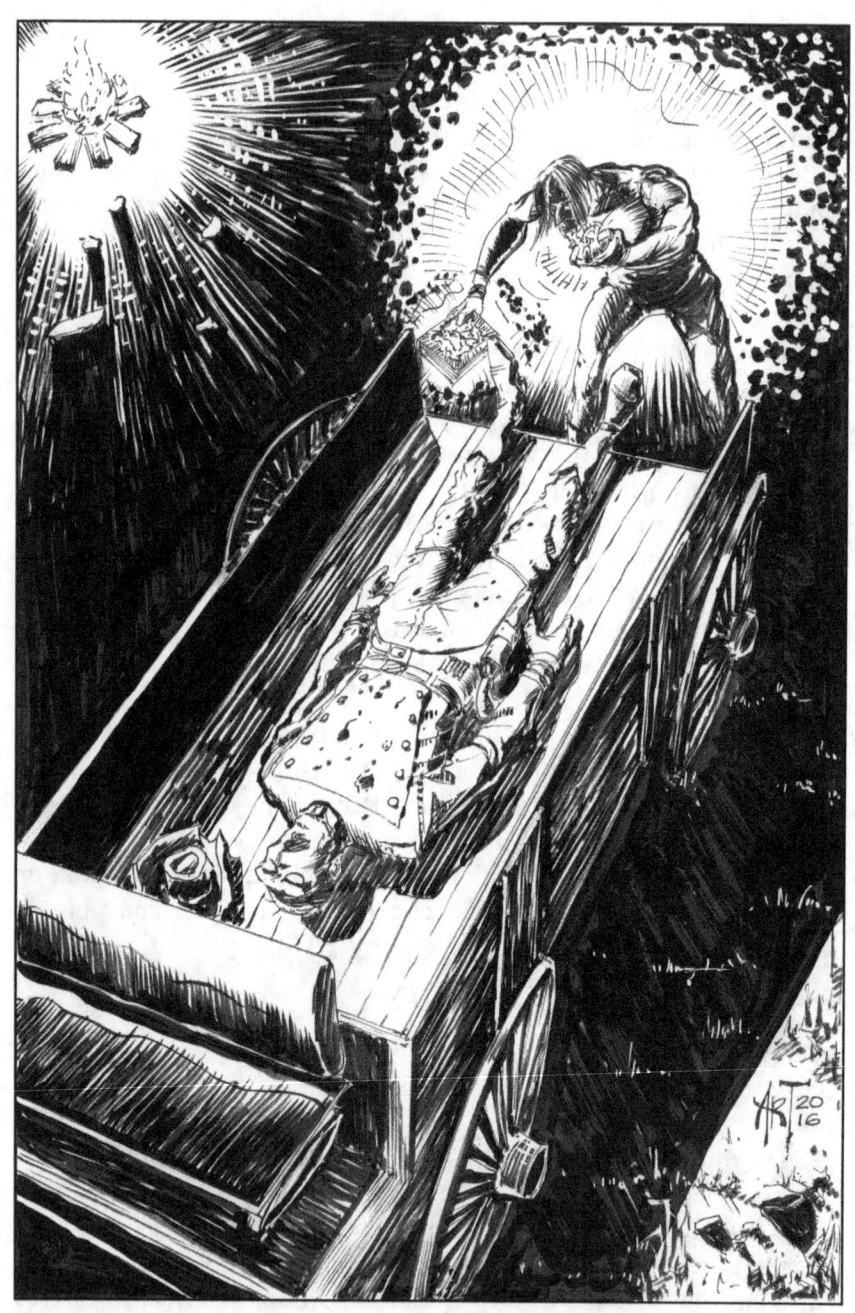

"You look terrible."

Finally, driven to the point of exasperation and near violence, Sam said, "Shut the hell up."

"What? You mean me?" O'Malley said.

Sam turned to stare at the writer.

O'Malley shut up.

For maybe five minutes. Then he started up again, commenting on the buzzards and the heat and the skull of a cow, bleached white by the sun and the wind. Sam sighed and tried to ignore him. When they reached the Drummond town line, Sam could have leaped from the wagon and kissed the earth.

He hid the wagon in the same spot he used the night before, close to the back of The Lucky Horseshoe. As he uncovered the wagon and walked the dead man out of it, O'Malley actually stayed quiet, observing in a manner that was both respectful and cautious.

Finally, speaking softly, the writer said, "Look at him."

Many of The Dead Sheriff's wounds had closed up. And several of them were still open and oozing that thick black sludge that filled up the body. Sam thought of it as magic blood. Whatever it was, it kept the dead man going. Experience had taught him that some of those wounds would get smaller as the day went on. And some of them would never close. The Dead Sheriff was running down. Sam wasn't sure how many more gunfights that smelly son of a bitch had left. It didn't help that his clothing was shredded and stained. He hadn't figured out how to make the magic take care of the laundry, so somewhere along the trail, some newer clothes would have to be found.

Constable Nicholson's office was three blocks past the St. James's establishment. The casino was closed up. A few onlookers chatted near the building, until they took notice of The Dead Sheriff. Sam wondered what happened to the man who had tried to cut his throat, the one O'Malley had pole-axed. Sam hoped he died from his injuries.

On the way to the constable's office, Sam ran through all the possibilities: Nicholson wouldn't be there; He was there, but would refuse to pay; He would delay the payment for some bullshit reason; He would try to arrest Sam and the dead man.

That last one had been tried before. Sam was confident in his ability (okay, the magic's ability) to get them out of the situation, but he hoped he didn't have to use it. Lately, it tended to wear him out and leave him with a hell of a headache. It didn't take a lot of mojo to walk The Dead Sheriff around. If he had to make him talk or shoot, then Sam's skull was apt to split open. The whiskey he had polished off last night hadn't helped.

As it turned out, despite all his worry, Nicholson was waiting for him with the gold. He wore a clean shirt and had a fresh shave. The shirt was a little tight, making his round gut even more prominent than it had been the night before.

"Got it all counted out for you, Mister Dead Sheriff," he said. Sam was standing just inside the entrance to Constable Nicholson's office. He'd left the corpse parked just outside the door. Nicholson peered around the edge of the door to address The Dead Sheriff. Sam sighed. Nobody wanted to deal with the fucking Indian.

"Give gold to Cheveyo," Sam said.

Nicholson squinted one eye and squirted a long string of tobacco juice onto the floor.

"I reckon that'd be okay," he said reluctantly.

The pounding in Sam's head sped up. Don't force me to do The Voice.

"If Dead Sheriff have to tell you, him get mad," Sam said.

Constable Nicholson swallowed and his face paled. Sam watched the man's large Adam's apple work up and down, and he thought Nicholson must have unexpectedly swallowed a nice, thick string of his tobacco.

"It ain't no problem." Nicholson's voice was thick, like he had suddenly developed a bad cold. "No problem at all."

The constable carefully placed the gold in a little wooden box. He handed it to Sam, who almost dropped it. The son of a bitch was as heavy as a fat whore.

"Need any he'p with that?" Nicholson said this with a shit-eating grin plastered on his ugly face.

"No," Sam said. He walked out of the office, determined not to let the strain show. He made the dead man lift his arms in a perfect cradle for the box. Making the corpse carry the gold only slightly increased the pain in his head, which was better than the pain he would have in his back by the time they got back to the wagon.

Then Sam remembered O'Malley, who trailed slightly behind the dead man.

"Hey, writer. Want to carry the gold for a bit?"

"Of course!" The tall man hurried forward to relieve The Dead Sheriff of his burden. "I'm most happy to help."

O'Malley lifted the box from the corpse's arms, and to Sam's chagrin, carried it easily. In fact, he caught up to Sam, and when he spoke, his voice was free of strain.

"Why do they call you Cheveyo if your name is Sam?" he said. "Who was The Dead Sheriff before he died? How do you....make him do those things? What is that necklace?"

"Forget you heard anything," Sam said. He resumed walking.

This was what he got for showing a tiny bit of gratitude, for allowing another person to share his food and campfire. Now, the idea of riding with O'Malley and letting him write a book about The Dead Sheriff seemed more trouble than it was worth. O'Malley couldn't print the truth, anyway. Besides, Sam wasn't going to tell him...

Those pale hands reached from the open hole and the fingers opened and closed, opened and closed, like the dead man whose face was still covered by dirt was fighting to remain in the cold, silent grave...everything. In fact, Sam had decided to tell him nothing at all. O'Malley was pissing him off with his continuous babbling.

So many goddamned questions. Sam's past was all he had (if you didn't count the money he had stashed away) and he wasn't going to share it with this scarecrow from back east.

The headache roared back with a vengeance. The writer kept pace with him, but he kept silent, for once. Perhaps Sam's words—or his expression—cautioned O'Malley to hold his words for a while. Whatever the reason, Sam didn't care. He was thankful for the blessed quiet. All he wanted was to go back to the camp and nap in the shade (and maybe take a little nip from a bottle) until the headache went away. Then, they would mount up for Damnation. Once he took care of business there, Sam decided to take a vacation. A nice long vacation.

Chapter Sixteen

Reverend Skaggs looked up at the sky, its heavenly blue, clear and cloudless, and declared it a glorious day, indeed. A light breeze cooled the crowd gathered in the small city park, if you could call it that. There was very little actual grass, but it was neatly trimmed. Standing on the bandstand, the reverend drew in a deep breath and thought; *this is as good as it gets in West Texas.* He was glad he decided to hold the service outdoors, under the glory of the Lord's heaven beaming down on him, blessing—anointing—his ministry, his word, and his influence over the townspeople, which had gathered to hang on his every word. Skaggs had a pretty good idea it would be the last time he addressed the faithful of Damnation. A bigger and better destiny awaited him.

Tugging on the chain, Reverend Skaggs pulled his watch from his pocket. It was noon. He stepped to the edge of the bandstand and raised his hands. The milling crowd grew still.

"Welcome, friends!" His voice boomed through the park. If he had learned anything in the past few years, it was how to manipulate a crowd. They wouldn't respond to a soft voice. They would reject any hesitancy or flicker of doubt. Years ago, Skaggs learned to give it to them loud and hard every time.

"Lord, bless these good people who have come out today to bask in your love and generosity. Can I get an Amen?"

The crowd Amen-ed right on cue.

Reverend Skaggs chuckled. "It does my old heart good to see you. We gather today, united in our love for Jesus, and in His love for us, each and every one of us. We're all sinners, yah know. Jesus knows it, and he still loves us. Can I get a Hallelujah?"

The shouts from the assemblage weren't as lively or as loud as he liked, but that was okay. Before he was finished, he would have them screaming like a three-dollar whore on payday.

"Friends, we are united in another cause, too. We have come together to take a stand against Evil. That's Ee-vill, with a capital E, brothers and sisters. Oh, yes. Someone is comin' to Damnation, and he wants to spread his Ee-vill to every corner of our fair town. He wants to make our fine, clean, little city live up to its name. Are we gonna let that happen, friends?" A few shouts of "No" drifted up to the stage. Reverend Skaggs turned up the volume.

"I said, are we gonna let that happen?"

This time the response was thunderous.

"Ee-vill has a name." He paused. He loved seeing them hang on his every word.

"It calls itself The Dead Sheriff—an abomination in the eyes of the Lord. What man dares to come back from the dead without the blessing of our Lord, Jesus? And if this here Dead Sheriff wasn't raised by Christ, and if he's doing the devil's work, then who is he workin' for, my friends? Who is callin' the shots?" "Satan!" some of them called. Others shouted, "The devil!"

"Yes! Yes! It's Old Scratch, for sure. Mr. Lucifer, king of the fallen angels. He has reached up from the deepest, hottest pit of Hades to send his agent among us. Did you hear me, friends? A ranch hand for the devil hisself is comin' to town. Are we gonna stand for that? ARE WE?"

The shout that rose from the audience was almost palpable. Skaggs was stunned by the intensity of it, actually staggering back a step from the edge of the bandstand. Yes, by God, this was what it was all about. He had created a need among his flock, sprinkled with a little fear. Now he would fill that need. And after this Dead Sheriff character had been torn to tiny pieces and planted back into the ground, folks in Damnation would talk about Reverend Ludlow Skaggs for a hundred years, praise Jesus.

Damnation? Hell, he'd be a legend all over Texas.

Right on cue, Sheriff Halwell stepped to the bandstand, faced the crowd and shouted, "What will we do, Reverend Skaggs? You have to help us."

Skaggs sighed. Halwell delivered his lines with all the feeling and emotion of a hitching post. Skaggs raised his hands again.

"I can help," he said. "Only because God has shown me the path upon which we must tread, and Jesus has shone his holy light on that path."

Several Amens flew up from the audience. Reverend Skaggs smiled.

"I can feel your love, brothers and sisters. I can feel this…this bond that has formed between us. Yes! It is strong. So strong. Together we will vanquish Satan's ranch hand. We'll send him back to that fiery pit faster than you can say 'Praise the Lord'!"

Suddenly, one of the men in the audience flew up into the air, screaming as he somersaulted through the air, his long hair swinging in circles, until he landed on his head. Skaggs was stunned into silence, until he saw the cause of the man's distress.

A massive man was shoving through the crowd. He struck a woman with his shoulder, sending her to the ground. He gave her no more concern than would a man swatting a fly.

The man was Nelson Frye, and he was in an all-fired hurry about something. Now the crowd noticed him, drawn by the screams of those Frye had bowled over. They parted for him, and the big man rushed to Halwell, who stood gaping with his mouth open.

Frye whispered something to the sheriff, bending nearly double to put his lips to the smaller man's ear. Halwell turned pale, and he swallowed several times. Skaggs heard him mutter, "Fuck me."

Halwell climbed up to the bandstand. Reverend Skaggs knew that the message Frye delivered was bad. Real bad. Sweat trickled down Skaggs's back.

Halwell squeezed up close to Skaggs, too close for the Reverend's comfort. He could smell the whiskey on the sheriff's breath. He'd probably had a couple of shots to calm his nerves before he delivered his big line in front of the crowd.

"What the hell is it?" Skaggs whispered.

The first time Halwell attempted to deliver the news, he couldn't speak. Nothing came out but a squeak.

"Spit it out, dumbass."

Swallowing again, Halwell finally managed to deliver the message.

"It's The Dead Sheriff. He's here."

Aware of the stares of the crowd, Reverend Skaggs managed to curtail the response he wanted to give. His heart hammered in his chest, and he felt it skip a beat.

"Who saw him?" he softly said. Keeping his voice low was the most difficult task he had ever attempted.

"Johnny Macklin got it from one of the stagecoach drivers. He saw them a few minutes ago, a mile or less outside of town, coming in from the east."

The staccato rhythm of his heart quickened.

This was it. He was about to face down either a fake or something that proved the existence of the supernatural, of an existence beyond life. Either way, Skaggs planned to come out on the winning end. He would ponder the philosophical implications later, if at all. Now his priority was to make sure the plan was on schedule, then regain control of the crowd.

"Is everyone in place?"

"Sure, sure," Halwell said. "I'll be on the mercantile with Woody."

"Then get going. You need to be there five minutes ago." "Okay, yeah." Halwell blinked stupidly three times before he jumped from the bandstand, stumbled in the dirt, and began a clumsy run to the edge of town. Halwell ate very well these days, and Skaggs wouldn't be surprised if his heart exploded like a stick of old dynamite before he reached the mercantile.

The onlookers were no longer merely curious. Outright fear showed on many of the faces. Those who weren't flat scared were confused, at best. Reverend Skaggs stepped to the edge of the bandstand.

"So y'all saw our Sheriff light out of here like his tail was on fire." Clasping his hands together, Reverend Skaggs leaned toward the crowd, as far as he dared without toppling off the bandstand.

"I have warned you. I have done my level best to prepare you, praise God. Now the time is here. The abomination walks among us, friends. Satan's hand-picked minion is here. The Dead Sheriff has come to Damnation."

He reveled in their gasps and cries. Several of those in the crowd grabbed loved ones and strangers for comfort. What he hadn't expected was the look on their faces.

Anticipation. Delight. A lust that was almost carnal.

Yet, Ludlow Skaggs suffered a moment of doubt. Had he gone too far? Should he have been less insistent that Armageddon was to be fought right here in Damnation? What he saw in the eyes of his parishioners frightened him a little.

And just like that, his doubt evaporated. Of course he did the right thing. He always did the right thing. The zeal of his followers would carry the town through the battle. When Reverend Ludlow Skaggs emerged victorious against the forces of evil, the people of Damnation would sing his praises, and that song—that legend—would carry him to Dallas and beyond. It would bring him wealth beyond imagining. And if Ludlow Skaggs had any notable quality, it was one hell of an imagination.

"Follow me, then. Come and be the soldiers in God's Army. We got us a fight today, friends. I won't lie to you. It's gonna get ugly, but our faith will see us through. It's time to blow The Dead Sheriff back to Hell!"

Chapter Seventeen

FROM THE JOURNAL OF RICHARD O'MALLEY:

We walked into Damnation.

It was the middle of the day. Sam (it was so hard not to call him Cheveyo; he hadn't explained the sudden change in names) left the wagon in a copse of scraggly trees behind a small rise just outside of town. I was hot and hungry, having ridden all morning. Sam said the day was actually pleasant for West Texas. To me, it felt as though we marched toward the gates of Hades. The "pleasant" temperature was far more brutal than even the worst summer day in Boston. Later, I would realize how tragically close my allusion was.

I hoped the apprehension of this fugitive would be fleeting. Though I craved adventure, and had begun to think of myself as a man who was acquainted with danger, I was, nevertheless, filled with a sense of dread. The closer we came to the edge of town, the greater the swell of my unease.

It was as if Damnation radiated fear like a campfire gave off heat.

Sam never acknowledged it, but I believe he felt it as well. The set of his jaw, the clenching and unclenching of his fists, the way he rolled his shoulders—they were all evidence of stress, a stress I had not detected in this young man prior to today. Even back in Drummond, when events were at their most dire, Sam had never caved to fear.

This foreboding was most odd.

Each step seemed like a footfall on a treacherous mountain pass, with only jagged death waiting below. How could this trek to a large Texas town in the middle of a bright day make me feel as though I were about to step into the abyss?

I was determined to shove these emotions to the side.

The Dead Sheriff walked stiffly in front of us, trudging like the marionette I now knew him to be. Though I understood why we couldn't simply drive the wagon through town and haul the undead avenger from the back like a load of fire wood, I wished for more riding and less walking.

"Why don't you get him a horse?" I said.

Cheveyo—Sam—shook his head.

"Too much trouble. What if the horse got spooked by a rattler and ran off with our boy? I'm up shit creek, then."

I mulled that over for another hundred yards or so.

"Give him a dead horse," I said.

Sam stopped so suddenly a swirl of dust was kicked up by his moccasins. He stared at me with no malice on his face. It wasn't an expression that resembled fondness, either. It was essentially blank, a look I would come to associate with Sam's frequent intervals of contemplation. For a young man who often acted with rash impulsiveness, he tried to take a moment to think things through.

He turned away from me to glance at The Dead Sheriff, who had stopped when we did.

"Couldn't you guide the horse the same way you do 'our boy'?" Sam had not explained this magic to me, at least not yet. I was confident he would get around to it, once I gained his trust. Still, I was getting an idea of how he did it. Apparently, the locket and book were the key. He kept the book hidden in his saddlebag, but I caught a glimpse of it two nights previous, as he held it, presumably to heal some of the damage that had been inflicted upon The Dead Sheriff at the casino.

Sam did not answer.

The town of Damnation grew larger on the horizon. It was much bigger than Drummond. From a distance, I would describe it as a growing town with dreams of grandeur. Many of the buildings were three-story structures, with one or two even taller. The dominant structure in town was an imposing church. It would not have been the tallest building in Damnation if were not for the enormous cross atop the steeple. It towered over the rest of the town, casting a long shadow; I'm sure, at certain times of the day. The church was easily as wide as the stable used by the police and public works department in Boston. It wasn't as fancy as some of the churches in my hometown, but it was larger.

Seeing that church only served to worsen my trepidation. Perhaps the anticipation of more bloodshed had put me on edge. It seemed I was not yet the hero I wished to be.

The edge of Damnation appeared to waver in the shimmering desert heat. The sparse, hellish wasteland suddenly became acres of buildings. A crowd had gathered on the far side of a wooden arch. The arch was painted white, and hanging from the upper curve was a large sign. On it was written:

WELCOME TO DAMNATION
THE FRIENDLIEST LITTLE TOWN IN TEXAS.

Sam made a sound, a small laugh perhaps.

I pointed at the people waiting for us just beyond the town's boundary. "Are you often greeted by such an audience?"

"Nope, and judging by them, I don't think they're here to hand out medals."

Sam read their mood correctly. As we were now near enough to discern individual features of the men and women, I plainly observed that this gathering was somber and full of dread. No one smiled.

No one, save for the older gentleman who stood in front of the others.

He was not very tall, yet he carried himself with a regal air, a man accustomed to leading others. He appeared to be well past sixty years aged. He wore an ill-fitting blue suit that was stained with blotches of sweat. Despite the beads of water bubbling over his forehead, his thin white hair seemed to stay in place, composed, slicked back with some sort of oil.

We stopped on the desert side of the wooden arch. The Dead Sheriff stepped forward until he was slightly in front of us.

The crowd barely drew a breath.

All eyes were trained on us.

Murmurs slowly rose from the crowd. More than a few women clenched the arms of their male companions.

The man in the blue suit stepped forward, outstretching his arms toward us.

"Welcome to Damnation, my friends." The voice boomed from his chest, sounding as if it came from a man twice his size. It was obvious this was a man used to addressing large crowds. He must be a politician, I thought. Most likely the mayor of this town. "How may we help you?"

For an instant, I marveled at the idea that the whole town would turn out to greet strangers. But the truth was that the crowd had not gathered for strangers at all. They knew why they came: to see with their own eyes what the legends and stories had told… of the devil that walks among men.

Despite hearing Sam's whispers, I started when the dead man spoke.

"I'm here for Nelson Frye." The words echoed, carried over the crowd by gusts of wind that began to swoop in from the small hills behind us.

The short man's smile was replaced by a look of puzzlement.

"Frye, you say? I don't think I know a Frye." He turned to the crowd. There were at least two hundred men, women and children gathered in the street. They did not appear to be dangerous. Still, I could not help but wonder if The Dead Sheriff had enough bullets to hold back this mob. "Any of you folks know anybody in town named Frye?"

Two men shook their heads. The rest of them continued to gape at the undead avenger.

"Tell you what," the short man announced in his expansive voice, "you all come on over to the hotel and rest for a bit on the front porch. They got chairs with pillows so soft you'll think you're a baby again, sittin' on your mama's lap. Then I'll fetch the sheriff and see if we can't find this feller you're lookin' for."

"Who are you?" I asked.

"Me? I'm just an old country preacher. Name's Skaggs. Ludlow Skaggs." He faced the assembly, lifting his hands above his head and waving them. "Y'all back up now. Make room. It's time to show these men the fine hospitality of Damnation."

The crowd obeyed the minister. Not only did they move, they dispersed, disappearing into alleyways and the buildings along the hard-packed dirt street.

Though Reverend Skaggs faced us once more, he walked backward, urging the three of us with hand gestures. "This way, boys."

"This is odd," I whispered to Sam.

Sam pinched the bridge of his nose. He looked tired. "Let's just get this over with," he said. "Stay out of the way and let me take care of things."

We moved further into the town. Under the fierce midday sun, sweat flowed from my every pore. It ran down my back and sides, and into my eyes. I wiped a sleeve across my face and discovered Reverend Skaggs had halted.

We stood in the center of the dusty street. Two-story buildings stretched for as far as I could see, containing the type of businesses you would expect to find in a town: a barbershop, a bank, and laundry, a saloon and so forth.

Aside from the four of us, the streets were deserted.

Panic struck me.

"Do something!" I cried to Sam.

He whispered again and The Dead Sheriff stepped closer to the minister. The short man did not flinch or falter. In fact, his smile grew wider.

"I want Nelson Frye."

Reverend Skaggs nodded. When he spoke, his voice no longer roared like thunder. It was pitched softly. His brows came down, shadowing his eyes, though the smile remained, as he began to speak in a near whisper.

"You know what I want, you evil piece of shit? I want to be the richest, most powerful man in Texas. I just have to show people I'm a problem solver. All you need to do right now is stand there and help make my reputation."

I heard the clapping of footsteps on the rooftops above us.

The Dead Sheriff's hands twitched.

Skaggs peered at The Dead Sheriff. "Damn, boy, if that's makeup, it's the best job I've ever seen." Skaggs scrambled to his right until he was under the awning of a storefront with a barrel of nails by the door.

When the minister next spoke, his voice regained its force and volume. "Halwell! Do it!"

From above, a hellish thunder filled the air. Before my eyes, The Dead Sheriff seemed to explode.

Many years ago my father had taken me to a patch of farmland outside of Boston. Police officials, officers and their families had gathered to watch a former soldier in the Union army demonstrate the police department's latest purchase. I could never forget the unique racket of a Gatling gun. The cacophony I heard that day was the blended chorus of several of the rapid-fire weapons.

Gatling guns had been placed on the roofs of several buildings, and Reverend Skaggs had led us into the field of fire. Instinctively, I dived to the ground and scrambled on my hands and knees to a narrow alley beside the hardware store.

Sam managed to get The Dead Sheriff to draw his guns, even as the walking corpse was hammered by the slugs from what I now believed to

"This way boys."

be four Gatling guns. The undead avenger twitched and jittered. Bits of thick, dark fluid flew from the exit wounds. The Dead Sheriff was coming apart.

Standing behind the corpse, Sam was covered with the black fluid. He seemed to be frozen in shock. I was reminded how young he truly was.

"Sam!" I shouted. "Move!"

Like a medium coming out of a trance, Sam shook his head. He turned to the side of the street opposite me. As he tried to reach shelter, I saw the first bullet strike his chest. The projectile exited through his back in a spray of scarlet. A second shot dug an angry furrow across his brow. Sam crashed to the dirt street.

The Dead Sheriff had taken so much fire I could see daylight stream through the holes in his torso. After Sam collapsed, the undead avenger was a puppet without strings. He crumpled to the ground.

Another volley of shots pushed the corpse around for a few seconds until the shooting ended.

The Dead Sheriff had been stopped. Sam was probably dead.

I had to escape.

I turned and crawled through the alley toward the back of the buildings. I emerged into another street, filled with one-story buildings and small houses. I resolved to hide in one of them until nightfall, then slip out of Damnation. I felt like a coward, but I convinced myself that there was nothing I could do for Sam, even if he still lived. Nothing except die. And I discovered that I really wanted to live. I wanted to see my mother's face again and feel the bracing winds of a Boston winter.

"Where you goin', asshole?"

The speaker was a stout man, gone to flab. He wore a suit, a bowler hat and a big silver star. He blocked my path.

"Are you the law here? Are you aware of the travesty of justice that has just occurred?"

The man laughed. "I hate you fancy-talking fucks from back east. Frye, give him a little taste of Texas justice."

A man of incredible size stepped from the corner of one of the buildings. He must have been close to seven feet tall with shoulders as wide as that of three normal men. He pointed a rifle at me, flipped it around and slammed the butt into my forehead.

The pain was excruciating. My vision was replaced by a blast of white light, as bright as the noon sun.

I never fully lost consciousness, even though there are stretches I cannot clearly remember. I recall loud voices and being dragged across rough ground. At one point, I entered darkness and was sure I was dead. It turned out that I had merely been taken inside one of the buildings and was out of the brutal sun. The pain in my head kept me from opening my eyes. I was aware of others inside the building and of movement near me and of the strong smell of sawdust. When the pain finally subsided, I opened one eye. Though my vision was blurry, I saw I was lying on a floor. Metal bars were a few inches from my face. It was a cell. I was in jail.

Conflicting emotions tore at me. I was ashamed at my predicament, yet relieved that my father could not see me. At the same time, I wished that fierce bulldog of the Boston Police Department was here to rescue me.

But I was alone. There was no rescue coming, unless I affected it myself, and that did not seem likely. I closed my eye, hoping the darkness would quiet my racing thoughts. Finally, I rolled onto my back and sat up. My head felt like a great weight soldered to the floor. I cradled my forehead in my hands, gasping as I made contact with the abrasion the butt of the rifle had left upon my forehead. When I regained my strength enough to open my eyes again, I realized I was not alone in the cell. Sam was stretched out on a cot.

His shirt was spotted with blood. Chiseled into his forehead was a deep, wet groove. Remarkably, he was still breathing. I stood up, but the weight of my throbbing head dropped me instantly to my hands and knees. I took a breath and waited for the room to cease spinning, then I crawled over to the cot.

When I reached Sam, I lifted his shoulder as gently as possible and examined his back. Blood pooled beneath him on the canvas surface of the cot. I didn't need to see the wound. It was obviously large, and it was still open. I removed my shirt and tore off one sleeve. I folded the material and pressed it to the wound. I hoped the pressure of Sam's body would keep the makeshift bandage in place and staunch the flow of blood. His condition was serious and, if untreated, certainly fatal.

I staggered to the front of the cell. Grasping the bars to keep myself upright, I studied the small jailhouse. Other than the single cell, there was a desk, two chairs and a rack that must have held rifles. The rack was empty.

The desk was clean save for my wallet, and Sam's leather book and amulet.

"Hey!" I shouted, hoping someone passing outside would hear. "We need a doctor in here! This man is dying!"

Silence was the only answer.

Chapter Eighteen

everend Ludlow Skaggs, Halwell and Frye stood staring at the putrid remains of The Dead Sheriff. There were a few other folks gathered along the street, all keeping their distance. Skaggs knew the townspeople—his sheep—would eventually show up for a peek, and that was fine with him. In fact, he was counting on it.

"Sumbitch is dead now," Halwell said, spitting tobacco juice near the dead man's ear, though he was aiming for the oozing black void where an eye had been. Frye watched with no expression on his face. Skaggs decided that the man was only truly alive when there was violence to be done.

Halwell kicked the gun still clenched in the fist of The Dead Sheriff. He had to kick it twice more before it came free from the dead man's fingers.

"I'll have somebody get a cart and haul this mess over to the town dump. We'll burn it tonight," he said.

"Oh, he'll burn," Skaggs said. "Just not at the dump."

"What do ya mean?"

"Get your men to start dragging wood to the center of town, right across from the hotel. We need a pole, too. About seven feet tall."

Halwell wasn't the fastest draw in town, much less a quick wit. But in a few seconds, it all came together for him and a broad smile broke out on his face. "Oh hell, yeah. We gonna have a bonfire."

Reverend Skaggs nodded. "The town heard the shootin'. They can see the corpse. Yet, if they believe the story, this lawman can rise again. So tonight we'll put the period on the sentence, praise the Lord. We'll send this ole devil back to hell."

"Uh, Reverend, what about them others? The Injun and the red-headed easterner."

Now it was the Reverend's turn to smile. "Boys, I say conspirin' with Satan is almost as bad as bein' the devil. Wouldn't you agree?"

Halwell nodded. Frye appeared to have not heard the question.

"Better make that three poles," Skaggs said. "And we're gonna need more wood."

Chapter Nineteen

FROM THE JOURNAL OF RICHARD O'MALLEY:

It was nearly dark before anyone came into the jailhouse. The man was young—younger even than Sam. He carried a rifle slung over his shoulder like a soldier in a parade. But he was too young to be in the military. He was too young, and his posture and appearance were too sloppy. He was accompanied by an elderly man carrying a leather valise.

The kid unlocked the cell door with a key he took from a drawer in the desk. He aimed the rifle in my general direction. I could smell liquor on his breath. "You behave now, boy. Doc wants to look at you and the fuckin' Injun. What's the point, I say, considerin' what's about to happen, but I just do what I'm told." Then he smiled.

Despite his advanced age, the doctor seemed sure-footed. He took my chin in one hand and inspected my face.

"That's a nasty bruise and cut," he said.

"Rifle butt." My throat felt dry and swollen.

"Your lips are cracked. How long has it been since you had water?"

I shrugged.

The doctor addressed the young man with the rifle. "This man is dying of thirst. Fetch some water."

"But I'm supposed to keep an eye on him." He laughed. "'Sides, he'll be real thirsty in just a while."

The doctor stepped out of the cell. He continued walking until he was inches from the other.

"You want to tell Skaggs you let this man die before his big party?"

The boy's expression darkened. "I'll get your goddamn water. If he escapes, it's on you, Doc."

He stomped to the door and left the building.

"I'm thirsty, sure, but..."

"Shut up," the doctor said. "Skaggs and his henchman are going to burn you alive tonight, along with the corpse of that other one." He reached into his valise and produced a Derringer. He thrust it at me. "Here. Hide this."

I shoved it in a pocket of my pants.

Burn us alive? The room began to spin again.

"Come here," the doctor ordered. He was kneeling next to the cot. "Turn him on his side."

I shook my head to clear it. That only made the room spin faster. I stumbled to the cot. I rolled Sam to one side. The doctor used a pocket knife to cut away Sam's shirt. He grunted when he saw the wound.

The young man returned with a tin cup of water. He handed it to me, but the doctor grabbed it away. "Get me a pail of water," he said. "And I need bandages. Get a sheet from the hotel. It better be clean."

The kid swore, rolled his eyes, and scooted out of the jail.

"Sam's pretty bad, isn't he?" I said.

The doctor pulled a rolled bandage from his bag.

"I wanted that boy out of here," he said. "You need to leave, too. Damnation is a diseased place."

"Why are you here?"

The doctor pressed a folded bandage against Sam's wound. He wrapped another bandage around Sam's chest and tied it off so it wouldn't shift. He didn't look at me again until he had finished.

"This was my wife's hometown. She loved it here, when it used to be a decent place. That was before Skaggs and his band of thugs showed up. The man has turned a fine little city into a whorehouse." He wiped his bloody hands on a small towel from his bag. "My Ada has been gone for six months. I think it's time I moved on as well."

"What about Sam?"

"The bullet went clean through," the doctor said. "He's lost a good bit of blood, though I reckon he'd get better, under normal circumstances."

"Under normal…"

The door opened, and two men entered. The kid was in front, followed by a short fat man in a striped shirt whose face glowed with feverish expectation. The fat man carried a Colt Peacemaker, which he constantly waved back and forth.

"Hope you got him all patched up, doc," the kid said, "'cause the fun's about to start. Oh, sorry about that water you asked for. There just ain't time."

The doctor—whose name I never learned—closed his valise and faced the two men. He made eye contact with each of them, then he said, "Johnny Macklin, Heath Buchman. I was there when your mamas squeezed you out."

"Yeah?" the fat one said.

"I regret not dashing your brains against a rock when I had the chance."

The two of them shared a glance before they shared a laugh. Finally, the fat one stuck the barrel of his Colt in the doctor's face.

"I could drop you right now, you old piece of shit, tell Halwell you was helping the prisoners escape."

"Leave him be," I said.

"Heath," the doctor said, "did I ever tell you that you were born with the smallest cock I ever saw on a baby? I know I told a lot of other folks in town."

Heath Buchman's face reddened. He pulled the trigger. I watched the back of the doctor's head blow across the room. The blood and bone smacked against the wall and began to slide to the floor in rivulets of red and white.

I sat down hard on the floor of the cell.

"Holy shit," Macklin—the kid—said. "You fuckin' murdered Doc."

"You wanna shut up right about now, Johnny," Buchman warned. His face was still flushed, and the fever in his eyes burned even brighter.

"Yeah, okay, but we gotta get these two out to the preacher. You wanna take the Injun? I'll get the other one." Macklin waved his rifle in my direction.

"The Injun is out cold," Buchman said. He whined like a petulant child. "I can't carry him by myself. You gotta help."

Macklin looked at me and rolled his eyes again, though he was careful to keep his voice neutral. He didn't think it was wise to cross his murdering friend. It was the only smart thing Macklin did that night.

"Shore, Heath, I'll help. You get one arm and I'll grab the other. You back up against the wall, feller."

I scooted until I felt stone against my shoulders. Macklin kept his rifle pointed at me as the pair of them dragged Sam from the cot. When they cleared the cell, Macklin kicked the door shut with his foot. He set his rifle on the floor to dig the key from his pocket. He locked the cell door.

"Be back for ya in a couple of shakes," he said with a smile.

"Hope you like the heat, boy," Buchman added.

They carried Sam to the street, laughing as they departed.

I was left with the body of the doctor.

The scream exploded from my chest. It was a primal wail against the injustice I had witnessed and the cruelty one man could inflict upon another. I did not know if anyone could hear me, nor did I care.

I came to the West to tell the story of The Dead Sheriff. Now that story was at an end and my tale as well.

I felt the weight of the doctor's small Derringer in my pocket. He had given it to me in the hope, however foolish, that I might escape. And what if I did? What kind of man would I be if I left Sam to suffer the indignity the minister planned for him?

I glanced at the room again, the body of the doctor, and the desk and chairs.

In that bleak instant, I knew what I must do.

The door opened again, and Macklin came in. His rifle pointed at the floor and the odor of liquor was stronger than before.

"Time to go," he said.

He unlocked the cell door, and I slowly stood, displaying the slumped posture of a defeated man. The illusion required very little acting.

"March on out of there."

I stepped out and Macklin fell in behind me. Before I reached the door, I halted. Macklin, in his drunken state, filled with the lust for violence, could shoot me on the spot. I was counting on his fear of the minister to keep me alive for a short time longer.

"May—may I ask a question?" I said, with a quaver in my voice.

"What?"

"Is my friend still alive?"

Macklin chortled.

"They ain't lit the fire yet. They're waitin' on you, hoss."

"Good." I pivoted, raising the derringer I had palmed in my large hand. I squeezed the trigger. The small bullet drilled into Johnny Macklin's left eye. The eyeball popped like an overripe grape. Macklin said, "Fuck." He folded at the knees and fell on his face.

I stepped over his body to reach the desk. I grabbed Sam's amulet and the leather book. It was as if other hands guided my actions, as if I, myself, were possessed. I did not understand how Sam used these things. In fact, the only thing that was clear to me was this: the one chance to escape this fate rested in those arcane objects. My hand burned when I touched Sam's property, an invisible fire that jumped from the book and necklace to my hand, then burned its way to my brain.

All the fear and doubt I had felt were obliterated. The only thing left was a fierce anger, quickly boiling into rage.

I stepped through the door into the night.

Chapter Twenty

Skaggs watched Halwells' men tie the Indian to the pole on the far right. The shredded corpse of The Dead Sheriff was hanging from the center pole. It had taken a lot of rope to secure the bastard. Parts of him kept falling off, for Christ's sake. Not to mention the corpse smelled like a dead skunk that had been curing in the sun for a couple of days. Torches had been driven into the hard earth in a rough circular pattern around the execution site. Their flickering light cast odd, elongated shadows. The heat from the flames kept the evening's coolness at bay.

Where was the Macklin boy with the easterner? Skaggs wanted to get this show on the road. He shook his head in disgust. Surely the quality of hired hands would go up when he got to Dallas. The thought made him smile. Of course it would. This night would ensure that. Ludlow Skaggs was about to become a legend in Texas and, soon, the rest of the country. He was the man who cleansed the world of a great evil. He took on the tool of the devil, and he won.

Now he just had to finish it—the period at the end of the sentence, as he liked to say.

The crowd was with him now, almost every soul in Damnation had turned out to watch the big show. The massive pyre dominated the center of the wide main street. Parents stood on each side of the street, laughing nervously with their families, sharing expectant glances with one another. They needed this. Skaggs needed this.

So where was that goddamn Johnny Macklin? That fat, little fuck, Heath Buchman, finished tying the redskin to the pole, as he held the unconscious Injun upright.

"Buchman," Skaggs said, soft enough to keep his words from carrying to the crowd, "haul that fat ass to the jail and find out where your buddy is."

"He ain't my buddy," Buchman said. The boy had a note of sass in his voice. Probably feeling the fever of the impending execution. Skaggs simply stared at him. After a few seconds, Buchman looked at the ground.

"I'll go fetch him, Rev'ren," he mumbled.

The need for fetching disappeared as the tall easterner walked out of the jail.

Reverend Skaggs wondered briefly what happened to the Macklin boy. His curiosity vanished as the tall man grew closer.

In the tall man's hands were a book that looked like a Bible and a silver necklace. The lips of the easterner moved silently. This didn't bother Skaggs as much as the strange glow in the tall man's eyes.

And the dark shape that appeared above his head. Darker than the night itself.

It had swelled into existence a few feet above the easterner, looking like nothing more than a small cloud. It quickly expanded; sprouting shapes that resembled wings and legs. Many legs. And it continued to grow.

A lesser man would have pissed his pants right then and there. But Ludlow Skaggs had steel in him, and whatever trickery was being conducted here would not change his plans.

Halwell and Frye stood behind him, unlit torches in their hands.

"Frye, get out there and deal with that cocksucker," Skaggs said. "Halwell, get that fire goin' now."

Chapter Twenty-One

FROM THE JOURNAL OF RICHARD O'MALLEY:

At this point in my narrative, I must confess that what follows may not be completely accurate. For a time, my perceptions were… altered. It all began when I picked up Sam's book and amulet. My fear and anger had been amplified, channeled into something greater than any emotion I had ever felt.

I walked through the door and into the street, heading toward a ring of light that engulfed Sam and The Dead Sheriff where their limp bodies hanged, tied to posts. I saw the minister and knew he was screaming orders. The sounds of Damnation seemed very far away, muffled and converging into a kind of singular beat, a maddening pulse that grew ever louder in my mind. Then, within that beat, a voice rose…

Say the words.

It came from within me, yet it was not from me. It was the voice of someone—something—strange.

And I trusted it completely. I understood its purpose—its command. It wanted the same thing I did. All I had to do was surrender. Let it consume me and take charge.

So I said the words that appeared unbidden in my mind, strange syllables that bore no resemblance to any language I knew or had ever heard, and suspected was not of an earthly tongue.

He held the unconscious Injun upright.

I felt the change come over me. I was an empty vessel being filling with a great power. The voice, I now know, came from the book. Through my rage, I ushered its wrath into me.

The memory of what happened next remains incomplete, like a dream half remembered.

That is, perhaps, for the best.

The last clear memory I have is of the chubby man with the badge lighting a torch, and using it to set The Dead Sheriff on fire.

Chapter Twenty-Two

Wake up, son, you wake up now!

All Sam wanted to do was sleep, but Old Luke wouldn't let him.

He tried to keep his eyes closed, to embrace the darkness.

Then, he smelled the smoke.

He came to instantly, and remembered where he was.

Damnation. There was gunfire. The pain in his shoulder and his back was excruciating.

Sam tried to move, but he was tied to something. He looked down and saw the wood. Much of it was kindling, freshly cut since there wasn't much use for a fireplace in West Texas. There was also scrap wood on the pile, some of it painted or covered with letters. Scrap from old buildings.

He turned his head to the left and saw the cause of the smoke. The Dead Sheriff was tied to a tall pole. He was on fire and in a minute or so, Sam would be blazing, too.

Old Luke came back: You just had to get one more bounty, didn't you?

He wished he had never stolen that damn book and amulet. He should have taken a horse instead and ridden north until he could go no farther. All that cash wouldn't do him much good now.

Above the crackle of the flames and the popping of the burning knots in the wood, Sam heard a commotion. The crazy preacher and the rest were watching someone walk down the street. Someone tall.

Sam swore.

It was O'Malley, and there was something wrong with him.

Chapter Twenty-Three

Frye calmly approached the tall man. Everything Frye did was calm. Skaggs wasn't sure Frye had ever known fear, which was a little disturbing, though it made him a good one to have on your side. Frye tapped the handle of his torch against his free hand as he walked. The torch hadn't been lit, and the top of it was dark with a smear of pitch. Even though Frye wore a gun, he didn't seem to think he would need it to deal with the easterner.

Skaggs gazed at the odd cloud or spider or whatever it was that floated over the tall man's head must have been some kind of—what did they call it—optical illusion. It disappeared for a few seconds and now it was back. He called Heath Buchman over to look at it.

"What do you see over his head?"

Buchman squinted.

"The moon?" He smiled at Skaggs, hoping to please.

"You don't see a dark cloud that kind of looks like a big ole spider with wings?"

"Uh..." Buchman's face scrunched up in concentration. "Do you see it, Rev'ren?"

"What?" Skaggs said. "No. Of course not."

The easterner stopped about fifty feet from the circle of torches. His lips still moved and he clasped the book to his chest. He had slipped the fancy necklace over his head. The medallion dangled about where his heart should be.

A soft wind kicked up, making the torches flicker. Skaggs heard the wood snapping from the flame, and he smelled the smoke. If he didn't move soon, his suit was going to smell like roasting flesh. But he was rooted to the spot, watching the tall man and Frye. What transpired before the reverend seemed mystical, and although he perpetrated the illusion of believing in the good Lord and the sweet Hereafter, Ludlow Skaggs was more of an atheist than he would he ever admit publicly. What he saw before him shook him to his crooked roots and paralyzed him.

As Frye approached the easterner, he took a two-handed grip on his torch and swung it at the tall man's head. The tip of the torch stopped a few inches from the stranger's skull. The torch broke in two. The tall man did not sway—didn't even seem to notice. He kept mumbling his silent prayer as his eyes burned with a deep, white-blue light.

Frye tossed the broken half of the torch to the ground and pulled a long revolver from his holster. He held it close to the tall man's forehead. When he pulled the trigger, Skaggs heard the roar of the gun, but nothing happened. At least for second. Over the easterner's head, one of the legs from the black mass extended, wrapping around Frye's head. With a quick jerk, and the pop of bone separating from bone, the head separated from Frye's body. The headless corpse stood for a second, blood spewing in a fountain from the open neck, before it fell to the dirt.

"Goddamn!" Heath Buchman said. "Goddamn, did you see that, Rev'ren? Did you see it? His head just disappeared!"

That wasn't what Reverend Skaggs had witnessed. Not at all. Oh, Frye's head had disappeared, that was certain. But it had been ripped away by something monstrous, something that the good Reverend would have sworn could not exist.

For the first time in his life, Ludlow Skaggs actually felt the need to pray, but the words would not come.

Chapter Twenty-Four

"There goes my bounty," Sam mumbled as the head of Nelson Frye was torn off by…

What the hell was that thing floating above O'Malley?

Sam didn't know what that Boston beanpole had done to the book and amulet, and he didn't have time to examine the situation. He had his own problems. The dead man was fully engulfed in flames, and the smoke was starting to choke Sam.

He tried to move his arms and found a little play in the ropes. He was held to the post by two loops, one just below the shoulders, and the other above his wrists. Whoever secured him to the pole must have thought there was little chance Sam would revive before he was burned alive. He rolled his shoulders and flexed against the ropes, every movement met with a thousand burning needles around the gunshot wound. But the ropes began to loosen. The acrid smoke—filled with the thick scent of burning flesh—seared his nose and throat. He turned his head away and drew in a deep breath of fresh air. Then, holding his breath, he went back to work on the ropes. The loop around his wrists seemed to offer the greatest chance of freedom. He clenched his fists, pulling his wrists upward. Sam bit off a cry of pain. The up-and-down action with his wrists loosened the rope enough for him to pull his hands free. He lost a little skin, though that was nothing compared to what would happen if he didn't escape the flames. He tugged at the rope around his shoulders, finally pulling it far enough from his body that he was able to push it above his head, ignoring the bolt of pain that shot through his upper body.

He was free.

He pushed away from the pole, and discovered his legs wouldn't hold him upright. He tumbled forward, sliding down the small mountain of wood, throwing sparks into the air. His flesh burned in a hundred places, and he fell until his momentum threw him into Reverend Ludlow Skaggs. The preacher squealed like a child. Sam might have screamed as well, if the impact hadn't made the world go gray and murky for a few seconds. When he could see again, he was on his back. The preacher was scrambling away on his hands and knees, emitting a small series of screeches. Sam was positioned so he was looking up at the flaming corpse of The Dead Sheriff. He clearly saw the dead man tear free of his bonds and step down from his funeral pyre, a fiery nightmare walking through Damnation.

Chapter Twenty-Five

Skaggs thought it was The Dead Sheriff who had landed on him. If it had happened just moments earlier, he would have been concerned that someone heard his scream. Now he just hoped to escape this night alive.

From both sides of the street, women (and a few men) screamed. Reverend Skaggs thought they were merely concerned for his safety. Until he rolled over. Alerted by the moving shadows and the growing heat he felt on his cheeks, he saw a nightmare come to life.

The Dead Sheriff, who had nearly been cut to pieces by the Gatling guns, was free. He was ablaze with the searing flames of Hell, and Skaggs knew he was looking for vengeance.

Skaggs climbed to his feet and backed away from the burning corpse. Halwell appeared by Skaggs's side.

"Do something," Skaggs shouted.

Halwell's eyes were transfixed on the burning dead man, wide with fear. Skaggs thought he looked like a cow caught in a thunderstorm.

"Kill that evil fucker," Skaggs blurted out, spittle flying from his mouth, and a trickle of urine running down his trousers.

Halwell took a step forward and emptied his pistol into the blazing form of The Dead Sheriff. The bullets had no effect. They just seemed to disappear into the flames bursting from the chest. The dead man threw his burning arms around Halwell. Skaggs watched as the slow-witted lawman's body ignited and burned before his very eyes. The screams pierced his ears, and the good reverend knew right then those were the screams of souls in perdition.

Skaggs turned to the crowd, his sheep. Some fled. Others could not move, seemingly wanting to follow their reverend to the slaughter.

"Help me," Skaggs implored them. "Lead him to the edge of town. Some of you need to get up on them buildings and fire the Gatling guns."

They began to move, just not in the direction Skaggs had ordered. The citizens of Damnation were slipping away from the siren song of his sway. They fled, abandoning Ludlow Skaggs, the man who had given them a prosperous existence.

This wouldn't do.

Skaggs would lead the agent of Satan to the edge of town by himself, if he had to. He'd man the guns, as well. History would shower him with rightful adulation as the man who killed The Dead Sheriff. Nothing was going to change that.

He turned and took his first step toward the city limits.

Then the earth opened beneath him.

Chapter Twenty-Six

Shaking and pale, Sam shoved past two teenage boys trying to escape Damnation.

He saw the dead man kill the local sheriff. Was all this O'Malley's doing? All Sam knew for certain was that he had no control over what was happening. It was time to scamper.

He heard a deep and frightening noise rise from beneath his feet. With a rumble, the very earth opened up between him. He leaped to one side and witnessed the creation of a fissure three feet wide and growing. The breach in the street appeared to be quite deep. As he studied it, something moved deep in the ground.

"Shit!"

Sam ran past the burning dead man and headed for O'Malley.

Someone stepped directly into his path.

It was the preacher.

"Will you help me?" the man said.

If Sam had a weapon, he would have happily killed the man.

Instead, Sam kicked him in the balls.

The preacher fell on his side, cradling his nutsack.

Sam scrambled down the street.

The black shape above O'Malley's head grew. Now it had too many legs to count and silver sparks sizzled around each leg. O'Malley's eyes turned silver, and more of the sparks flew from them.

The flock of Damnation screamed. Wood cracked as buildings collapsed with a reverberating thunder and storms of dust. Fires erupted as torches kissed lumber. But nothing compared to the grinding sounds that came from deep within the street.

The fissure had widened, and new openings appeared. Sam ran faster, giving O'Malley a wide berth.

Another sound stopped him. It was a wet, slithering noise.

Keep going, he told himself.

But in biblical fashion, he stopped to look. The temptation was too great.

Chapter Twenty-Seven

That cock-sucking injun had kicked him in the nuts.

He rolled in the street, waiting for the worst of the nausea to pass. He climbed slowly to his feet, dimly aware of the screams and the unmistakable odor of roasting flesh.

The Dead Sheriff stood only a few feet behind him, a man clasped in each of his burning hands.

And that wasn't the worst of it.

Ludlow Skaggs realized he was straddling the crack in the ground, and the crevice was getting wider. He did a little jig, hopping to his left. He had always been fast on his feet, literally as well as figuratively. He knew when to seize an opportunity, just as he knew when to cut bait. The time to slice the line had arrived. He could still head to Dallas and try to make a go of it. Perhaps he could no longer be the hero of Damnation. He was already constructing a story in which he was recast as the survivor of Damnation. He could get a lot of mileage from the sympathy.

All he had to do was get out of town.

He probably could have done just that, had the shadow not appeared from the tear in the ground. As he stared at the black shape seething from the hole in the earth, Skaggs realized it wasn't a shadow. It was something much worse. Black and shiny, wet with some vile slime, the thing looked like the tail of a massive dog, or an arm without a hand. The end was tapered, and the entire thing was covered with bumps, dark domes that seemed to throb.

The goddamn thing grew before the reverend, making the night sky blacker. Twenty, thirty, then forty feet long, it propelled itself straight up into the sky, wavering slightly, as if stroked by a desert wind. Skaggs tore his gaze away. Dozens of massive tentacles popped up across the length of the street.

The black tubular shape in front of him rippled as the many bumps on its flesh opened up to reveal mouths—hundreds of mouths full of sharp teeth.

Reverend Skaggs had time to scream once before the blackness descended upon him, and the mouths began to feed.

Chapter Twenty-Eight

Sam watched the preacher disappear into the darkness, and felt a calm as he heard the man's trailing, fading shrieks.

"Sweet Jesus."

He didn't know what the black things were or where they came from. He just knew they didn't belong here—in Texas or in this world.

Sam watched O'Malley stand in the street, silver eyes sparking. The book was clasped to his chest. His other hand held the amulet. Sam couldn't look at the hovering cloud above O'Malley's head. Something about it hurt his head.

Sam slapped O'Malley's face. The tall man's head shook from the blow, but he didn't wake up. Sam slapped him again, harder. O'Malley moaned.

Sam grabbed the leather book and pulled it from O'Malley's grasp. It burned like a hot coal. Sam cried out, and dropped the book on the street.

"Ch-Cheveyo?"

"It's Sam. Time to go."

As O'Malley blinked stupidly, Sam risked a glance above his head. The dark cloud had vanished.

"Dear God," O'Malley said.

Down the length of the street, the black tentacle things scooped up dozens of people. The air was filled with screams, and the wet chewing of a thousand mouths.

Sam picked up the book. Though it was still very warm, he could hold it without blistering.

"I'll explain later," he said. "If I ever figure it out. Come on."

He pulled on O'Malley's arm. The tall man allowed himself to be led away. Within a few steps they were both running for the edge of town. With the wooden arch in sight, the ground started to shake again. The pair passed under the town sign just before it fell down. They continued running for another twenty yards before they both realized that the ground outside of Damnation wasn't quaking.

They stopped and looked back at the town. The buildings at the edge of the city shook until they fell apart. A mighty wall of dust was thrown up by the collapse of the structures, preventing the two men from seeing the aftermath. But they could hear the sounds of destruction and the deep, resonant rending of the earth.

Long moments later, the dust settled. The only light came from the pale moon.

Not a single building remained. In fact, save for the occasional wooden plank, nothing was left. Sam didn't see a single person, not even a corpse.

Damnation had been wiped from the earth.

The two men stood in silence, too shocked to speak.

Sam didn't know how much time passed before O'Malley shouted.

"Look!"

Something moved in the wasteland that had been Damnation. It was a figure, growing closer.

"What is it?" O'Malley said.

Sam squinted. It took a minute, but finally he recognized the charred remains of The Dead Sheriff. Tendrils of smoke trailed from his blackened body.

"A fucking bad penny," Sam said. "That's what it is."

Chapter Twenty-Nine

FROM THE JOURNAL OF RICHARD O'MALLEY:

It has been six days since Damnation was swallowed up by the Texas desert.

We rode hard for a night and a day before we stopped for food and rest.

Sam told me in unbelievable detail what he witnessed. He was unaware of the great power present within the book and the amulet. He once again wears the odd medallion around his neck. The book is stowed away with Sam's gear. He hasn't examined it since that night. For myself, I wish to never see it again.

We're heading north. Sam is allowing me to tag along for now. I am no longer certain I will write that book. I still feel The Dead Sheriff can be a force for good in the lawless West. I'm not sure Sam agrees.

But I am certain I will stay. That night in Damnation changed me. I am no longer a stranger in this journey. Somehow, Sam and I are now connected to The Dead Sheriff.

Things have changed.

Last night, I awoke, shivering. In my sleep, I had kicked away my blanket and the night was cold.

Sam slept on the other side of our dying fire.

But someone else squatted on his haunches next to the flames.

It was The Dead Sheriff.

He would never pass for a living man, but the power in the amulet had erased the damage from the fire and the Gatling guns. Seeing him lit by the small flames, looking as though he were a living man, perhaps lost in thought, I remembered Roger Ebbets, the cattle agent I had met on the train. It was remarkable that the encounter had occurred only a few weeks ago, when I was a different man.

Ebbets believed The Dead Sheriff had the power to show him an imminent death. Where Ebbets only saw a dark emptiness, I was filled with awe at a universe that could give birth to such a phenomenon. What other secrets did this walking undead man possess?

I sat up, wondering why Sam would have moved him to such a position. When I had settled in for the night, the corpse lay hidden in the wagon.

Then the dead man's head swiveled to look at me, and I knew he moved independently of Sam's control.

My breath caught in my chest as I studied the corpse's face, for something trailed down the cheek of The Dead Sheriff.

It was a single tear.

Chapter Thirty

Not every person in Damnation died that night. A few escaped and dispersed throughout the region, sharing the story of The Dead Sheriff's terrible wrath.

A few weeks later, a pair of riders arrived at the ruins of Damnation.

One was a massive figure on a large horse. His body was covered by a poncho and his features were hidden by a hat. The hands that grasped the reins were misshapen and were the color of bruised fruit. He didn't speak.

The other rider was a lean man. His red hair hung to his shoulders. From his mount, he surveyed the sparse remains of Damnation. He sniffed the air.

"They were here," he said.

His companion grunted.

"Magicks leave a residue, one that can be sensed, if you know how," the red-haired man continued. "This is the smell of my magick."

They rode the scorched earth until they reached what had been the edge of Damnation. Here, the desert was unblemished. The red-haired man spat on the ground.

"I'm coming for you, you son of a whore. And I'll take back what you stole from me."

The other rider grunted again. The two of them turned their horses to the north and rode away.

THE END

Afterword

It probably started with the Lone Ranger.

When I was a kid, westerns were everywhere, especially at our house. My dad was a nut for them. The table next to his chair always had a Louis L'Amour book on it. A John Wayne movie on a Saturday afternoon took precedence over everything else, even baseball games. Half the TV schedule was comprised of shoot-'em-ups, including reruns of the Clayton Moore Lone Ranger series.

Believe me, I grew up well versed in "Giddyup" and "Whoa!" and "Reach fer the sky, mister!"

At some point, though, I'd had enough. I developed interests of my own, and the stuff my parents liked couldn't be my favorites anymore. It just wasn't cool.

Among my growing passions were Chiller Theater, Famous Monsters of Filmland, Marvel Comics and pulp magazine reprints of Doc Savage and The Spider.

Years later, I came across a DVD of Lone Ranger episodes. Giving in to a twinge of nostalgia, I bought it. It wasn't great, but it was a classic part of my childhood. More importantly, it started the wheels rolling toward What If?

A lot of writers will tell you that almost everything springs from What If? My moment came right after the Lone Ranger and his stoic sidekick, Tonto, had stopped the bad guys, thus earning the undying gratitude of the whole town. As the crime fighting duo saddled up and rode off toward their next adventure, I thought What if everybody thinks the Lone Ranger is in charge but he's really just some guy hired by Tonto to be the face of their crime-fighting operation and later, after the Ranger is snoring in his bedroll, Tonto creeps back to town to collect the reward money that the Ranger always turns down? Hey, a guy has to plan for his future. Maybe Tonto needs a down payment on that retirement condo in Boca.

Something else writers will tell you is that the What If moment occurs maybe ten or twenty times a day. Out of those, maybe–maybe–one idea a week will become the germ for a story or novel or screenplay or poem.

The Tonto-as-boss notion was one of those that seemed to offer nothing more than a moment's amusement. Nothing to see here, it seemed to say, so move along. I did.

But every now and then, the notion would resurface and I'd examine it and toss it back to wherever the lonely, unused concepts reside. It was incomplete—one half of an equation. One day, during a marathon of bad horror flicks, the other piece of the concept fell into place.

The faithful Indian sidekick has a magic talisman that he stole. He only understands it enough to do one magical thing: to reanimate a corpse and control it like a puppet. While the rest of the West believes The Dead Sheriff is a murdered lawman that dug his away out of his grave to bring to justice the killers of his family, the truth is much different. The undead avenger is simply a means for a young man with a mystical totem to earn a little cash. Unfortunately, where magic and money are concerned, things inevitably go wrong.

Despite a tendency for bits of himself to fall off along the dusty trail, I plan for The Dead Sheriff to be righting wrongs for many years to come, and encountering the oddest characters to ever saddle up, like the crazed cannibal brothers, a traveling vampire bordello and the posse made up of the West's far less successful masked vigilantes. Did I mention the magic talisman's original owner and his demonic sidekick? Or the time traveler?

I hope you'll stroll into the saloon, belly up to the bar and order of a shot of pulpy fun. The Wild West is about to get very weird.

Mark Justice
In the hills of Kentucky

Acknowledgements From the Author

I wrote the first draft of this book during a particularly rough time, so first and foremost, I have to thank my wife, Norma Kay, for her unwavering support and encouragement.

My mother and brother have always been in my corner. It's a good feeling to know so many good people have my back.

Kudos also to Geoff Moore for his technical wizardry.

A special appreciation goes to Leigh Ann Heineman, director of the Highlands Museum and Discovery Center in Ashland, Kentucky, and their wonderful Civil War exhibit, "The Gathering Storm." Getting to play with actual firearms from that period was immensely inspiring.

THE DEAD SHERIFF LIVES ON

If that isn't the most bizarre essay title I've ever written, I don't know what is. And yet it fulfills its purpose and lets you know what the future holds for this series created by our good buddy, Mark Justice, a few years ago. I also felt, now that you've had the fun of meeting the Dead Sheriff and his companions, you should know a bit of the book's history and what lies ahead, God willing.

It was early last autumn of 2015 that Mark wrote me asking if Airship 27 Productions might be interested in taking on this Weird Western series. The first book, which you now hold in your hands, had previously been published by another outfit and although they had done a decent job with it, Mark wasn't completely satisfied with the results. I had the sense he wanted a more pulpish approach to character, one like we attempt to do with all our titles, i.e. dress them up with great art and colorful covers. As all the rights had reverted back to Mark, he was free to bring the series to another publisher. You can't possibly know how delighted I was that he'd chosen Airship 27 Productions.

Mark had been one of the first writers to contribute to our enterprise when it started up over a decade ago and I was always a huge fan of his storytelling talents. Now to get the chance to bring one of his most daring characters to our line was like getting an early Christmas gift. Mark went on to inform me that he'd begun work on the second Dead Sheriff novel and would continue to do more as long as we, and the fans, wanted them. Thus the deal was struck and we agreed he'd send us his revised manuscript early in 2016. Again, my excitement was huge. I knew instinctively this would be a special project for us and a winner.

Then the New Year rolled around and before any of us knew what had happened, Mark's heart gave out on him and he passed away. All of us who knew and loved him were shocked beyond words. There was a numbness clouding my thoughts those first few days after I heard the news and then the sadness set in. We had lost a truly wonderful and loving friend who could never be replaced.

I remember thinking about Mark's wife, Norma Kay, and the awful pain she must have been enduring. My wife and I found a condolence card, I scribbled a few words in it and we mailed it off. We both said lots of prayers in those days that whatever angels inhabit our earthly realm would be sent to comfort her throughout the days to come.

And somewhere in all that, we resigned ourselves that our plans for the Dead Sheriff would most likely never come to fruition.

Happily we were wrong on that count.

About a month ago I opened my e-mail to find a letter from Norma Justice. In it she told me how Mark had shared my enthusiasm about our plans for The Dead Sheriff and she was writing to see if I still wanted to proceed with those plans; exactly as Mark and I had agreed upon. In the coming weeks Norma, and their friend Brian Spears, were instrumental in locating Mark's manuscripts for both this first story and the portion of the second he had begun. Though I have not looked at it yet, wanting to devote my attention fully on this introductory book, it is most likely that some time next year, I will take it upon myself to read, edit and finish the second Dead Sheriff novel. It's something I owe my friend and want to do with all my heart and soul.

After that?

Well, being the Managing Editor of one of New Pulp's leading publishers, I'm connected to dozens of terrific writers; many who love this weird western genre and would take to the Dead Sheriff like a duck to water. So if all goes well, you can expect this volume to be a reboot that not only relaunches Mark Justice's amazing series but one that will continue long into the future. With your support and God's blessing.

Thus, the Dead Sheriff will live on. That phrase still cracks me up. To the point I can hear Mark up there laughing his glorious, beautiful laugh.

Thanks,

Ron Fortier

Managing Editor
Airship 27 Productions
4/29/2016

ABOUT OUR CREATORS

Author

MARK JUSTICE (23 Sept. 1959 – 10 Feb. 2016) was a writer, podcaster and radio personality. His published work includes *Deadneck Hootenanny, Looking at the World with Broken Glass in My Eye, Dead Earth: The Green Dawn* and *Dead Earth: The Vengeance Road* (both with David T. Wilbanks). He edited *Appalachian Winter Hauntings*. His short fiction appeared in four volumes of *Legends of the Mountain State*, two volumes of *Horror Library, In Laymon's Terms, Dark Discoveries, The Horror Garage, Dark Jesters, The Green Hornet Chronicles, The Phantom Chronicles Volume 2, The Captain Midnight Chronicles, The Avenger Chronicles, Damned Nation*, and he contributed to *The Book of Lists: Horror*. Mr. Justice produced and hosted the popular genre podcast Pod of Horror. He also hosted a morning radio show in Kentucky, where he resided with his loving wife, Norma Kay and their contentious cats.

Interior Illustrator

ART COOPER - is a Canadian artist/writer/editor who was a founding partner of Spectrum Publications, which published three bimonthly fanzines in the early '70s. Art was a member of the inaugural Cartooning program at Sheridan College in Oakville, Ontario, where the guest instructors included such luminaries as Joe Kubert, Neal Adams and Will Eisner. Art contributed to a number of fan publications and penciled two stories for Orb Magazine before getting married and completing his engineering degree. Art has worked as a project manager in the Mining and Metals industry for the past few decades, and has done some freelance advertising work on the side. Art is the proud father of two grown sons, and lives in Mississauga, Ontario with his current wife and daughter.

Cover Artist

ZACHARY BRUNNER – graduated from the School of Arts with a degree in filmmaking. Upon graduation, he realized that he would rather pursue a career in illustration, needing a more creative job than the high-stress environment of film production. He began working with comic writer Jim Krueger on two graphic novels, "The High Cost of Happily Ever After," and "Runner." "High Cost" is currently available at Amazon, "Runner," is expected out this year.

While studying at SVA, Zachary worked as a concept artist on an animated film called "Brother," directed by Sari Rodrig. The short film went on to win countless awards all over the world, having been shown at festivals such as Cannes and the Student Emmys. Zach currently is working on Sari's second short animated film, "Essence."

For the past year, he has also worked as a storyboard artist for Torque Creative, the in-house advertising agency for Mercedes-Benz. He is also currently working on several storyboards for short independence films.

Other print projects included "Christopher Rising," "Penny Dreadful" and "The Poisonberry Fortune" and "Foot Soldiers, Volume 1." He planes on furthering a career in concept art and in the comic book industry.

DEATHWALKER

TOUCHED BY DEATH

While on his vision quest, the young Cheyenne brave High Bird encounters the sprit of Death. The powerful wraith recruits the boy as his new agent in the world and High Bird returns to his tribe altered forever as Deathwalker. When the Cheyenne become the target of a vengeful Pawnee Shaman, Stands Alone, only Deathwalker can stand between this evil sorcerer and the total destruction of his people.

Writer R.A. Jones has woven a new and exciting fantasy set against a background authentic Native American lore and culture. He dares to imagine what this wild untamed land would have become had there been no conquests by outside civilizations beyond the great waters. Here is an old world re-envisioned in a bold new action packed adventure worthy of pulp writers such as Robert E. Howard and Edgar Rice Burroughs. Featuring stunning cover art by Laura Givens with interior illustrations by Michael Neno.

Airship27 is proud to present R.A. Jones' DEATHWALKER, another original and quality title in the New Pulp movement.

AN AIRSHIP 27 PRODUCTION

AIRSHIP 27 PRODUCTIONS – *Pulp Fiction For A New Generation!*
Available at Amazon.com and in PDF ebooks at Airship27Hangar.com

www.ingramcontent.com/pod-product-compliance
Lightning Source LLC
Chambersburg PA
CBHW070826250626
47170CB00006B/2223